ROPES AND TREES AND MURDER

Book Six: The Fiona
Fleming Cozy Mysteries

PATTI LARSEN

Cover design by Christina Gaudet
www.castlekeepcreations.com

Thanks, Kirstin!

ISBN-13: 978-1-988700-90-8

CHAPTER ONE

The fresh paint smell washed through the foyer as the open front door of the annex gaped, three workmen carefully balancing a large, leather sofa between them, muttering about care and caution as I stood to one side and watched them maneuver their expert way. Sunlight shone through the stained-glass panels flanking the tall, oak entry, casting a stunning light scape over the parts of the shining wood floor not covered in a temporary mask of cardboard laid to protect them from the heavy boots of the men unloading furniture.

Heart in my throat, I stayed out of the way, though not out of concern for the safety of either the expensive piece I'd added to the sitting room's décor or my floors but simply because, after months of waiting and planning and gutting and rebuilding,

Petunia's annex was so close to completion I could taste it. Maybe that was just the chemical mix of hardwood sealant and acrylic paint, but it equated to the same thing, right?

Shadows passed over the doorway, the tall, handsome figure of Jared Wilkens and his slim, stunning girlfriend, Alicia Conway, crossing the threshold. They both beamed at me while the workmen disappeared into the sitting room on my left, the attractive blonde inhaling and looking up the majestic, curved banister of the staircase toward the second floor, taking in the view as much as I had when I'd come here only a few minutes ago to oversee the unloading of the new furniture. I took a second to close my eyes, open them again, look around me as if for the first time and caught my breath.

"Oh, Fee," Alicia gushed, hurrying to me, her high heels tapping softly on the cardboard before clicking on the wood floor. She grasped me in a huge hug even as I mentally grumbled about the scratches her shoes were likely leaving and knowing I had to get over that surge of protectiveness. I'd be having guests soon enough and the floors would just have to live with it.

"Thanks for meeting us for the final walkthrough." Jared took his turn, embracing me quickly before he pulled away, huge smile lighting his handsome face. "Are you happy?" Was that real worry in his eyes when they met mine?

"You're seriously kidding me right now." I

punched him playfully in the upper arm before hugging myself in an effort to keep from squealing in excitement. They'd been through every step of the remodel with me, from the rearrangement of the layout to the selection of the flooring to the color choices and even the specific pieces that gave the annex its lush, unique look I loved. From the multi-hued hardwood to the white and dark cherry stairs with the heavy banister I couldn't wait to decorate for the holidays (yes, it was only May, but Christmas), the large crystal chandelier sparkling over our heads, the rich, delicious colors and exquisitely understated painting hanging over the front door to the individually adorned rooms with a new theme of seasons... "It's perfect, Jared. I can't thank you both enough for everything you've done."

"On time," he grinned at me, winked. "And on budget." Thank goodness for that, though I'd fretted the last month over my dwindling renovation account. Part of me worried he might have purposely eaten some of the costs to keep this project from running over. I knew Jared felt responsible in many ways for the failings of his father, my own near-death experience in this very foyer what felt like a lifetime ago. I hated to take advantage of him or his generosity, but, well. I'd find a way to make it up to both of them.

"Just in time," Alicia rolled her eyes and laughed. "If I had to field one more panicked reassurance for your mother, I think I would have lost it." She squeezed his hand as if to take the sting out of her words and he smiled that sweetly indulgent smile he always seemed to have for her as she grinned at me. "I'll be happy to let Aundrea know the annex is now ready for the wedding on Saturday."

She had to remind me. It was Monday already and I still had a ton of things to do, it seemed, before the big event in six days. Nerves jangled as I joined the adorable pair and took the next half-hour to tour the entirety of the space. The few new staff Daisy hired to set up the annex stayed out of the way while I did my best to enjoy the walkthrough, despite the growing sense of nervousness I had. Not for the space itself, that was taken care of. No, it was the impending sense of stress I'd bitten of a giant mouthful of holy crap what was I thinking that loomed over me and tickled my mind with the thought I really, really needed to recruit help beyond mere employees.

There were still a few details to take care of and I'd been so busy at Petunia's the last few months it seemed like we'd never finish. Busy enough I'd come to the realization this was far too much for me to handle alone. Sure, I could run myself ragged, would likely end up exhausted and cranky. I'd rather enjoy it, though. And while one of the people I wanted to approach for a partnership was readily available, the other wasn't exactly in the right frame of mind. Which made me hold off and catch my breath and worry all the more about what I'd done.

As I peeked in every space, fluffing pillows while Jared made notes about small things he wanted to address and Alicia used her critical eye for design to suggest minor alterations, I whispered a mental thank you to my best friend, Daisy, who even now hustled next door at my B&B, allowing me this time away to make sure everything was perfect.

I still had no idea what I'd do without her. And didn't want to find out.

"Thanks, Fee," Jared said. "I'll have the workers take care of the last few things the first of the week after the wedding is over and we're out of your hair. Then you should be good to go for the season." He paused at last at the front door after a quick tour of the garden. The landscapers were putting finishing touches on the flower beds, the hated fence finally down, the vast yard between the Carriage House, Petunia's and the annex feeling like an oasis now. The expansion of the koi pond and addition of a lovely stone bridge—Jared's idea—gave Fat Benny and his happy fish friends a chance for more of a world to explore, not to mention a few new additions to their threesome they seemed content to accept.

"I honestly can't thank you both enough," I said, felt my breath catch for the millionth time, realized I was so close to tears it surprised me. When I hugged them again my heart was racing and rather than let Jared off the hook with a quick embrace, I squeezed him an extra moment before whispering in his ear. "Jared." I couldn't speak for a second, felt him relax as he hugged me back.

"You're welcome," he whispered in return. And sighed like some inner tension finally left him. How much did he struggle with his father's misdeeds? How much of that did he take on himself every day? Enough, I was sure of it. When I met his eyes, Jared blinked a bit, flushed, looked away, but he was smiling and I giggled in delight at his response, unable to stop myself.

Alicia's fond expression turned teasing. "You really have to name this place now, Fee," she said. "The annex just doesn't do it justice."

Groan. "I know," I said turning to look back into the foyer, the bright sunlight showcasing the gorgeous interior in a way that made me want to go through this all over again next door. And kick myself for even considering it. At least, not without backup. "I will. I just... need the right name." There was time, and yet no time, really. This house was now booked fully until the end of September, and it wasn't even officially opened yet. Despite her now rocky mayorship, Olivia Walker's tourism push wasn't letting up any time soon, it seemed.

"It'll come to you," Jared said before smiling down at Alicia. "We should go." I turned back in time to see the faint frown between his brows, the way he glanced at his watch. "Fee's busy and we have that thing."

Alicia's face tightened before she sighed in a tight burst of exhale. "Right." She hesitated then glanced at me. When she reached for my hands, her grasp felt a bit too tight and for the first time, I noted the matching tension in them both. Because I was a crappy friend, and everything was about me.

Before I had a chance to ask them what was going on, Daisy blew through the front door, beaming a huge smile, her heavy, blonde hair swept into a stunningly messy bun at the base of her neck, her lovely blue dress hugging her curves, exuberant smile the most beautiful part of her. I found myself grinning at the expressions on the faces of the two women who followed in behind her, gesturing for them to enter.

Pamela Shard's eyes swept over everything, grin tight and gleeful. But it was her fiancé, Aundrea Wilkins, who literally squealed in excitement, rapidly hugging first her son and then his girlfriend before kissing me on both cheeks. She swept past me without a word, chattering to Daisy, hanging onto her arm, Pamela winking at me on the way by while my bestie gave the happy couple the tour.

"I guess I don't have to field any more questions," Alicia said. Laughed. She sobered a bit, hand still holding mine, though her grip was lighter, less tense. "Has Lucy changed her mind?" She asked softly, with caring, while my happy heart clenched, and I fought off a deep sigh threatening me. The partnership thought lingered as I answered.

"Not yet," I said, wondering if my mother would ever come around. Would return to the woman I knew I needed at my side if I was going to make this work. While she was no longer so desperately sad about her self-styled failure in January on that ridiculously stupid baking show and subsequent loss of confidence, she wasn't the mother I adored. Or the woman I could call on to take part in this project the way I knew would benefit both of us. Gone was the bubbly, cheerful and optimistically powerful Lucille Fleming I loved so much. Didn't help that Dad had continued to work cases in his new private investigation business. Not that I blamed him for Mom's unhappiness, but the two of them seemed distant for the first time and I worried constantly—when I wasn't working, that was, which wasn't much. So "constantly" really was a word I used to make myself feel better for forgetting about their troubles on a semi-regular basis (bad daughter). "I'm still working on her. So is Daisy." The fact not even my irrepressibly kind and adorable bestie—and yet, perfect partner choice #2 when all was said and done—couldn't reach Mom wasn't helping. "But the catering and the cake are covered, so things are on schedule." God, I was so tired of that word and laughed when I said it.

"I hear you hired Vivian to bake?" Alicia's tentativeness made me grin. Sure, we'd thawed a bit of our tensions since the Queen of Wheat helped me uncover the truth behind the murder of Ron Williams, but that didn't make us friends or anything. Still, I'd been low on options and Vivian French had been coolly professional when I'd approached her about taking over for Mom. Not a moment of judgment or a hint of the conflict we'd shared in the past showing. So, maybe we could co-exist in Reading after all without devolving again into a shouting match behind her bakery for the entirety of town to gossip over. We'd see. No promises.

"It'll be perfect," I said. "And nothing makes me happier than having the two of you as our very first guests." The entire annex was booked out for the wedding, and I had a few surprises for the young couple, including some extra-special pampering even the brides weren't going to receive. A small thank you, but they both worked so hard I wanted them to enjoy their weekend.

"I can't wait." Alicia giggled, both hands over her mouth, wicked look aimed at her boyfriend who cleared his throat, blushing all over again. They were so freaking young, seriously. Hard to remember that sometimes, but it was lovely to see them happy. And while I'd briefly considered the pair of them as possible partner choices, their continuing expansion of their own business made that a ridiculous idea.

Besides, I wanted Mom and Daisy and the more I thought about it, the more it made perfect sense.

Wait, there it was again, that tension in the young couple, as the slim blonde dropped her hands, both sliding over the front of her crisp black business suit. "Jared," she said, elbowed him not so subtly. "Just ask her."

His hesitation hurt, not because I worried what he might need, but because he would ever think I wasn't there for him. When his eyes met mine and he opened his mouth, I poked him in the chest with one finger. And in that moment, I decided no matter what if Jared Wilkins asked, it was an automatic affirmative from Fiona Freaking Fleming.

CHAPTER TWO

"Fee," Jared said.

"Yes." I grinned. "Anything."

He laughed, tension easing again. "You don't even know what I'm asking." Gratitude shone in his eyes, his hand reaching for Alicia's who beamed at me and held his in both of hers.

"I told you," she winked at him.

"Just tell me and I'm there," I said. "Any place, any time. Whatever, whoever, just name it." Again with the tears burning my eyes? Get it together, Fee. But I couldn't help it, not while these two lovely souls smiled at me like I'd handed them the moon all of a sudden. Sure, like they didn't do the same for me? For the first time my mind called them friends— not business acquaintances, not Pete Wilkins's family, but real friends. Made me want to hug them all over again.

I guess today was going to be an emotional day, then.

Jared cleared his throat, met Alicia's eyes before nodding and sighing, a big exhale, broad shoulders sagging just a bit as he leaned in like he needed to keep this between us. Sunlight crossed his cheek, shining over his stubbled face and for the first time I noticed he looked tired, drawn as if the afternoon's illumination highlighted how transparent he was becoming. Worry stung me deeper than I expected as he spoke.

"You've heard about the new zip line park opening near the equestrian center?" His voice pitched so low I almost missed half of what he said. I nodded quickly, fighting a frown.

"There's been some controversy, right? Something to do with an endangered woodpecker habitat?" Daisy was telling me about it just yesterday. The young couple who moved here to open it had gained approval from the council to go ahead but had run into issues just a week ago when some environmentalist group claimed a rare woodpecker species had their nesting site inside the park grounds.

Alicia's face tightened, eyes flashing, lips grim. "Jared's a silent partner on the project," she said. "Carmen and Aiden are friends from college." Jared looked suddenly uncomfortable, shrugged as she went on. "They were careful, Fee. They did a full assessment before they chose the site."

"Everything was supposed to be fine," Jared said,

sounding dull now, a bit defeated. He ran one hand through his thick, dark hair, shaking his head. There was that weariness again, aging him past his mid-twenties. How had I forgotten he'd taken on the weight of the world when he'd chosen to make right the sins of his father? This annex was hardly the only project he was working on. Had he stretched himself too thin? "I feel terribly for them. They worked so hard on this."

"Like you didn't." Alicia reached up on her tiptoes to kiss his cheek. "Anyway, it doesn't matter. They can protest all they want. There's no proof the woodpeckers are nesting anywhere near the park or are even this far north."

"Doesn't stop bad press though, does it?" Jared sighed again, hugged her against him, tucking her head under his chin. Dear heavens, could they be more adorable? Nope. "I'm still thinking we should delay opening, but they have so much invested—"

"It's not your fault," Alicia said with the kind of firm support that told me she really was the perfect partner for him. And had likely been shutting down his self-doubt for some time now it was so practiced. She didn't move out of his embrace, but her eyes met mine with unshakeable faith. "Here's the thing," she said. "They're doing a local's launch tomorrow, but Jared's worried no one will come because the protestors are threatening to shut down the opening."

Whoops. "And you'd like me to come," I said, "and show support, is that it?" Before either of them could confirm it, I grinned. "I'm in. What time?" Because I had the time. Well, I'd be making it, wouldn't I? Poor Daisy would just have to have my back.

Alicia lunged for me and hugged me tightly around my neck, lips on my cheek. "10AM. And thank you, Fee," she said. "I just know if enough popular locals attend, we can salvage this whole mess."

Jared's phone rang, his frown as he answered renewing my concern and I stood there, wishing I could help somehow while he stepped outside to talk to whoever had called. Alicia tucked in next to me, hand taking mine, as she met my eyes, hers fluttering, lashes damp.

"I'm so worried about him," she whispered, voice catching, free hand waving in front of her face to fan away her tears. "Fee, he's giving everything he has, and he never thinks it's enough. This means so much to us," she gestured at the annex, "and you do because it seems like you're the only one in this damned town who appreciates how much he does. How hard he works. You know." She swallowed. "To make up for Pete." She rushed on before I could say a word. "I wanted to leave, to just walk away and start again somewhere else, but this is home. He wants to stay. So, we stay. I just…"

I nodded. "I meant what I said, Alicia. Anything either of you need. Name it."

Her smile wavered but it was there. "He'll be okay. He just needs a break. This park was supposed to be fun, you know? A chance to reconnect with friends, a simple side project." She exhaled, sagged against me. "It just seems like he can't catch a break on anything."

Damn it. We'd just see about that. And while it was nice of her to consider me one of the popular locals—something I personally doubted considering my track record as a murder magnet—if she thought I could make a difference, then so be it. "I'm there."

Alicia bit her full lower lip while Jared hung up, staring down at his phone a moment while we watched. "Just be prepared," she whispered. "I think it's going to be a big protest tomorrow. So, we're not asking a small favor here."

Jared turned and joined us again, crossing the threshold, eyes dark and lips thinned. He tried to smile but it seemed like the sunlight did nothing to illuminate his once happy face. "We should go," he said. "Sorry to run, Fee."

"I'll see you both tomorrow," I said, giving him my best smile even if he couldn't answer in kind, because what were friends for? "10AM sharp. Can't wait."

His kind patience shone through, softening the edges of darkness that shadowed his face. "Thanks, Fee. I really appreciate it."

Seriously. This surge of protectiveness I was feeling all of a sudden? Those damned protesters had better look the hell out.

Aundrea and Pamela, Daisy firmly in tow, swept their way back into the foyer, Jared's mother bubbling over, her happy voice echoing as her heels clattered on my floors and I inwardly winced over then again. She hurried to her son and hugged him with great enthusiasm while Jared kissed her cheek. "Sweetheart," she gushed, spinning to look back into the annex as if she owned the place. "You did a fantastic job. It's *gorgeous*." She lunged for me then, hugging me tight, a far cry from the grim and unhappy woman I'd met the day after her hated husband turned up dead in my koi pond. How far she and Pamela had come, the pair of long-lost lovers finally able to be together. "I can't believe we're getting married here this weekend." When she beamed a smile at her partner, Pamela grinned indulgently back. While the newspaperwoman's expression wasn't quite as openly delighted as her fiancé's, Pamela's happiness was in no way diminished in my eyes.

I was surrounded by people in love, and that stirred up some things that reminded me I had my own chance at happiness lingering in the wings.

Thinking about kissing Sheriff Crew Turner? Enough to brighten any day.

CHAPTER THREE

Still chattering, Aundrea grasped her son's arm and dragged him with her, Alicia on her other side, while Pamela lingered, watching her love and the sweet young couple as they descended the steps to the walk on their way to the street. I inhaled the freshness of the spring afternoon, breeze from the open door soothing my worry, my heart, while Pamela met my eyes.

"Jared mentioned the park?" Leave it to her to bring that up at a time like this. Well, she was a reporter.

I wrinkled my nose at her. "I'll be attending the opening," I said. "Protestors or not."

She nodded once, dark eyes pale in the sunlight. I caught Daisy joining us out of the corner of my eye as Pamela spoke. "I'm prepping a story for this week's *Gazette*," she said, sounding amused rather than worried, so I released some of my growling protectiveness for Jared and Alicia while she went on. "Caused quite the kerfuffle in council, let me tell you." She winked slowly. "I guess you missed it?"

Whoops. "Not really paying close attention to local politics at the moment," I said without apology.

Pamela shrugged, hands in the pockets of her suit pants, squinting into the sun while Aundrea waved at her to come along, dear. "Olivia's hanging on, but I'm thinking there's a shift in power coming sooner rather than later."

While I didn't agree with all of our mayor's practices, I felt an odd affinity and loyalty to her. "She's done a lot for Reading," I said.

Pamela didn't comment on that. "Aundrea's been worried about Jared." The shift in subject made me start. "But he refuses to slow down. I wonder how long he'll punish himself for his father's failings." She sighed and her humanity showed, her own concern for the young man she surely adored if I read her endearing if fleeting expression correctly.

"I wish I could help," I said, feeling at a loss.

Pamela's quick, sharp smile as she leaned in, eyes narrowed in wicked focus, was all the warning I got. "You want to help, Fee? Write that damned column I've been asking you for." She left without another word, casual stride carrying her down the steps to Aundrea who hooked her arm through her fiancé's. All four waved and I caught myself waving back, Daisy joining me, the both of us in silence until they were gone, driving off in separate cars while I held my breath and let the afternoon sun warm my face, turning then to stare into the gorgeous interior of the annex. Clinging to the moment like it needed to last forever, blinking slowly into the quiet interior, letting myself truly enjoy what I'd made and now wanted to share with the woman standing next to me. I just had to convince my mother.

"Are you going to write it?" Daisy's voice sounded soft, subdued, and when I turned to her she wasn't looking at me but staring with her own quiet joy at the entry. She was as much a part of this place as I was now, and while her question could have been intrusive it instead made me grin. Did she have any idea what I wanted to ask her? I doubted it. I just hoped when the time came she said yes instead of worrying she wasn't good enough.

"Do you think I should write it?" I hooked arms with her, not wanting to move just yet, Daisy making no effort to leave, either.

"I do." Daisy ducked her head, tucking a stray piece of dark blonde hair behind her ear, grinning. When her gray eyes met mine, she giggled. "Don't you?"

I inhaled, exhaled. Shrugged. "We'll see." Okay, I was beaming again. "Daisy, *look*. Look what we did."

She laughed then, hugged me and I hugged her back. Before leaning away, wry smile sideways. "As much as I'd love to stand here and admire it forever," she said, "someone has an appointment to keep." She looked back toward the foyer again. "And I have guests to take care of."

She had to remind me. "You could go see Vivian for me." Weak, Fee. Really weak. Couldn't I just stay here in the annex and hide out for a while?

Daisy squeezed my hand before exiting, heading down the walk toward Petunia's. Her lovely voice reached me as she greeted a couple who'd exited a car parked in front of the door, luggage piling up on the sidewalk. The older woman's unhappy expression eased while Daisy welcomed them, though the mid-sixties gent in the matching khaki vest and floppy hat his companion wore looked my bestie up and down in a way that made my skin crawl. Just ew.

It did break my moment of pausing to absorb the silence of expectation hanging over the annex. Whether that was a good thing or not, it didn't matter. Okay then, back to work it was. And after the mixed bag of emotions I'd just been through, those same emotions still lingering and sifting through my mind, surely adding a short, business visit to the Queen of Wheat wasn't the end of the world.

With a blown kiss for the newest addition to my world, I closed the front door behind me.

CHAPTER FOUR

Margaret Peadley escorted me into the kitchen office at French's Handmade Bakery, ushering me into a chair as she sorted through a pile of paperwork on her desk. Vivian's right-hand woman grinned jovially while I relaxed in her happy company, her round, red cheeks and bright hazel eyes a huge relief.

"Vivian's out of state at another location," Margaret said, "but we're right on schedule with the cake and the catering support you asked for." She patted the pages in front of her, the design of Aundrea and Pamela's towering cake sketched out the way the couple requested. While the initial ask was theirs, it was up to me to ensure the bakery delivered. While I wasn't Vivian's biggest fan and wished Mom was in charge of the confections and the food in general, at least I knew my old rival was a professional.

A short few painless minutes later and I stood, final details perfected and heart lighter. At least this part was handled, if not by the one person I wished I could count on to do so. I wasn't sure if Margaret knew what I was thinking, but on the way out she paused at the door, hand on my arm.

"Please tell Lucy if she ever changes her mind..." she hesitated while I frowned a little. Right, Vivian made Mom an offer once, one that undermined her confidence further, as far as I was concerned. But wait, was it Margaret who made the untimely mistake? "I'd love to have her contract out for us. She's a brilliant baker, Fee."

That was a far cry from the supposed job offer of subordinate slavery Mom said Vivian suggested. And made me pause, rethink, while I hated doing so. Had my mother overreacted? No way, I would not let Vivian off the hook for making Mom feel inadequate. Still, I'd jumped on the Lucy Fleming bandwagon without actually hearing the full conversation between her and Vivian. Damn it, was I giving her the benefit of the doubt all of a sudden?

I left Margaret then, doing my best to hide my upset, hurrying up the street with long strides that carried me, not to Petunia's as I'd intended, but instead to the front walk leading to my parent's house. Traitor feet, I couldn't rely on them, it seemed. Nor did I stop myself from knocking, though, suppressing the knowing sigh that clenched inside my chest when I entered without being invited—home was home, no matter how old I got—and slipped off my shoes in the entry before drifting toward the kitchen.

There was a time when I couldn't wait to get out of this house and had for a long ten years. And then a time when I loved it, not so long ago, a time that I saw my parents in a different, happier light, when Mom and Dad's practiced comfortableness was a light I gravitated to. That's why every time I crossed the threshold the last few months frustration caught my breath and tugged at my feet, slowing me down. Not my job to heal them, but still. How could I give up on them when I finally found them again?

The moment I entered the kitchen I knew today wasn't one of those days where Mom could at least pretend she wasn't on the brink of a complete meltdown. From the tears on her cheeks and the way she glared at me while she wiped them away, I clenched against onslaught and held on.

"He's opening an *office.*" All of her disappointment and unhappiness and the struggles she'd been facing I could only guess at flooded her voice until I wanted to cry with her. "An *office.* Isn't that just *lovely?*" Mom turned her back on me, shoulders stiff, bowed. "Now everyone will know I bullied him into retiring and I'll look like a waspish old nag."

Okay, this was getting so out of hand I was going to shake her. "Mom, what are you talking about?"

"John." She snapped Dad's name over one rounded shoulder like that answered everything.

Well, I guess it kind of did. "For his P.I. business?" Wince. Mom's body shuddered like I'd hit her. "Mom, no one will think—"

"You have no idea how horrible people in this town are, Fiona Fleming." Mom spun back at me, jabbing a finger toward me, her face pinched with so much hurt my need to shake her turned to a powerful desire to wrap her up in a hug and keep her safe. Not from the folk of Reading but from herself. "They're already talking and now he's making it worse."

The most horrible part of all of this stupid, relentless situation that was taking my mother down a road I couldn't bear to watch her travel? There was nothing I could do to help her. Nothing I could say to take that look of self-judgment and recrimination from her normally lovely face. As I stood there, mouth opening and closing while I fought for a single word of support to give her comfort, I finally understood how far outside what she was going through I really was. And that if anyone was going to rescue my mom it had to be my mom.

Damn it.

The front door opened behind me, fresh air wafting in, the sound of steady, heavy footfalls at the entry turning to the whisper of sock feet on hardwood. Dad joined us, head down, his quiet, steady presence no match for Mom's unhappiness. She spun away again, arms hugging herself, refusing to look at him while he carefully kissed my cheek and met my eyes, his own full of the kind of buried sadness that hurt far worse than any overt show of pain.

"Hi, Fee," he said, deep voice soft.

"Hi, Dad." I hugged him, saw Mom twitch, watched her hurry away down the hall toward their bedroom, slamming the door behind her like me choosing to embrace him meant it was us against her. When I flinched, he sighed, patting my shoulder after he released me, leaning one hip on the counter. My dad had always seemed invincible to me, an immobile rock of a man, sheriff in this town for as long as I could remember. Solid, dependable, honest. Even when I was a teenager and we fought over my future, even when I couldn't bear to be here anymore because he didn't understand me—so I thought, little did I know just how alike we really were—I always respected and admired him for the kind of steady power he emanated. My dad was eternal.

How I hated to see the shift in him, the way he seemed reduced by Mom's struggle. As if her hurt was Delilah to his Sampson, her pain his Achilles' heel. Understandable, yes. Still painful to see. And I'd been so busy I'd done little, really, to help either of them.

Way to add guilt to the mix, Fee. Sheesh.

"Mom says you're opening an office," I said, trying to sound bright. "That's great, Dad."

He frowned, craggy line between his heavy brows pulling them together before he sighed deeply, a long exhale of frustration. "I only broached the idea this morning," he said. "She's a bit ahead of me, I'm afraid." He hesitated then, another glance at the hallway, a faint trace of longing on his face. "I'm actually thinking about giving up the whole thing, Fee. Your mother. Well." He cleared his throat, crossing his arms over his chest, staring at the floor while my heart broke.

"Don't you dare." I kissed his stubbled cheek. "This isn't about you or anything you've done or plan to do, Dad and we both know it. Mom needs to figure this out." I squeezed his elbow before chewing my bottom lip in anxious worry. "I wish I could just..."

He nodded. "Me too." Dad's eyes flickered to the hall again. "Me too."

The silence that stretched between us was just too much. "You're taking some cases?" Too sparkly by far, Fee, and so transparent I could see through it. Was positive Dad did, too, but his faint smile was grateful.

"A few," he said. "Just keeping busy." More pain.

"I'm sorry, Dad," I said, saying it at last, the apology I'd meant to share since I forced his hand in January. My eyes stung with unshed tears, my throat catching, nothing of the overwhelming joy I'd been feeling able to shut down this swing into sadness. I'd done this. I'd made him tell Mom what he was up to when she was so vulnerable, at a time she felt betrayed by the joy of her new venture, as unpalatable as the sabotaged cupcakes she'd served to the judges on that idiotic show. "This is my fault."

Dad hugged me again, familiar embrace steadying

me, holding me like he used to when I was little and needed comfort. Maybe he took some of his own from me hugging him back. I hoped so. Regardless, when I stepped away again, he cleared his throat twice before he brushed my bangs away from my eyes and kissed my forehead.

"No," he said, real smile finally appearing, "it was my fault for keeping things from Lucy. And from you, clever girl." Another kiss landed. The last of the lingering hurt I'd carried since the winter crumbled and disappeared as my father touched my cheek. I hadn't even realized I'd been hanging onto it. "Let me handle your mother. You have a lot on your plate." I tried to protest, hating he was right, but he was already guiding me to the front door. I slipped on my sandals and embraced him one last time as Dad rested his cheek on the top of my head.

"Love you, kid," he said. "Proud of you."

Choke. "Love you too, Dad," I said. Squeezed hard. "Rent a damned office already."

He didn't comment and I hurried away before I could cry into his broad chest, but when I glanced back, he was smiling so maybe, maybe I'd a least brought a bit of happiness to one of my parents.

CHAPTER FIVE

I should have gone back to Petunia's. I had a lot to do, prep for the wedding, guests to wrangle, emails to answer. And apparently tomorrow I was going to be busy, at least for the morning, supporting my friends the best I could. While Daisy wouldn't complain when I filled her in and was amazing and I loved her for everything she did... yeah. Petunia's was my responsibility (until I asked her otherwise) and I far too often left her holding the bag(s) without real benefit to her. Mind you, that would change when I convinced her and Mom to step into the roles I needed from them. But, despite that knowledge and the pressure it created, as I hit the street, I found myself turning left instead of right, the mid-afternoon sunshine begging me to linger just a little longer.

Sammy's Coffee bustled with tourists and locals,

the barista winking and giving me an extra pump of vanilla, asking after Petunia. I accepted the donut for the chubby pug waiting for me at home, refusing to ruin the girl's gift by telling her in no way, shape or form would the fawn beggar be getting a sniff of wheat and sugar if I had anything to say about it. I left with two cups and the brown bag in a cardboard tray, heading back up the street for my chosen destination. I'd managed to exercise and diet a few pounds from my inherited pet, hoping to keep Petunia the Fourth around for many years to come. Though the sweet-natured pug wasn't happy about the present state of her dietary restrictions (or the giant *DO NOT FEED THE DOG ANYTHING* sign I'd had to place at the front entry to prevent guests from sneaking her food), her happy-go-lucky nature hadn't faded with the reduction in horrific gas passing or the fact she didn't snore quite so loudly anymore.

I climbed the steps to the sheriff's office with a rise in optimism, slipping inside to the chime of the front doorbell and smiling at Toby Miller behind the reception desk. A firm fixture in her fleece vest and carefully styled hair, she grinned at me with a wave when I paused to smile back.

"He's in his office," she winked. "Go on in."

Nice to have a standing invitation these days instead of the former, more uncomfortable, state of affairs I'd suffered since returning home to Reading. Instead of being called into Crew Turner's office to be chewed out on a regular basis for poking my nose where he didn't want it, I instead found myself sneaking fairly frequent visits by choice.

While not the dating arrangement I'd been hoping for, Crew's company—and apparent delight with my appearance—reinforced my confidence our conversation in January about his intentions wasn't just talk. Though, how he was ever going to get over his wife's death I had no idea. Not my job. For now, I'd take a few stolen hours here and there over coffee in his office.

I crossed to the swinging gate that separated the bullpen from the main reception area, this place as familiar to me as Petunia's. I'd almost grown up here, visiting Dad more often than not while he was sheriff, so it felt natural to pass that border. I waved to Jill Wagner who waved back, grinning as she talked to someone on the phone. The glare from her desk mate wasn't lost on me, though I did my best to smile a winning beam of a screw you at my disgruntled deputy cousin. Robert Carlisle sneered back, eyes narrowing, that hideous 70's mustache of his making me queasy.

"Sucking up to the sheriff again, Fanny?" He snorted like he was funny. Not.

Snarly growl with a go to hell for good measure. "Don't you have work to do, Robert?"

"Maybe if you Flemings would mind your own damned business instead of stirring things up," he shot back.

What the hell was that supposed to mean? I paused to snap something highly inappropriate for the office that would require a string of curse words that likely would have singed the air when tall, dark and handsome leaned against the door frame of his office and interrupted.

"Deputy," Crew said in that deep, velvet voice of his, catching my attention and my breath and diffusing Robert's pathetic attempt to get a rise out of me. That single word sounded like a command. My cousin shot his boss a sullen stare before going back to his paperwork. I arched an eyebrow at the delicious jeans and khaki-shirted sheriff while his slow, lazy smile appeared. He stepped back from the door and waited for me to enter, closing it softly behind me, shutting out the rest of the world.

I leaned back against the glass, looked up into the bluest eyes I'd ever seen and inhaled his scent while Crew didn't move, didn't speak. The temptation to kiss him was so powerful I felt my hands tremble while he finally broke eye contact and helped himself to one of the cups nestled in the tray.

"Thanks," he said, voice rough around the edges. He sipped, eyes sparkling, like this was fun for him, teasing me. Especially since one of his ground rules for Fee and Crew was in full effect.

"I'm starting to regret our no kissing in the office agreement," I said, knowing my voice sounded husky but not caring really, not right then with him standing so close and looking like that, all yummy and broad-shouldered and everything.

Crew's deep chuckle wasn't helping any. He left my side and retreated to his office chair, while I repeated, "Down, girl," in my head a million times before I sank into the wooden one opposite him and handed over the bag with the donut. Crew grinned, took a bite, handed it back.

"Petunia will never forgive you," he said.

I took a nibble, a sip of my own coffee. "She'll never know." I sighed without meaning to, handing off the treat which Crew devoured without a word, watching me with those blue eyes like he knew I needed a minute.

I shook off my mood, still thinking about my parents, forced a smile. Crew and I didn't get a lot of time to talk so no way was I wasting it on something I couldn't change, and he couldn't help me with. "What's Robert's problem today, anyway?"

Crew shrugged, leaned back in his chair until it creaked, stretching out his tall, big-chested body before settling. "The usual," he said. Then made a wry kind of face, full lips twisting as he met my eyes. "Your dad's been making his life uncomfortable lately, that's all."

I was all for that. "And yours?" Okay, so Robert's unhappiness was fair game, but I'd done enough to make Crew's life kind of miserable since we met. I really hoped we'd moved past that, even though it was Dad and not me this time around.

"I'm good." Crew seemed amused rather than upset. "Let's just say some of Robert's assumptions about what he can and can't get away with when it comes to law enforcement have been challenged the last few months." How cryptic. "I think your dad went a bit easy on him when he worked for him. Family, you know?" Did I. Dad's sister wasn't exactly a charmer herself, though I saw little of Aunt Doris since she and Uncle Ray lived in New Hampshire these days. My most vivid memory? Her taking my favorite toy horse from me on my seventh birthday and giving it to Robert who proceeded to break it on purpose just to see me cry.

Yeah. She was a peach.

"And you?" I grinned around the rim of my cup.

There was that sexy chuckle again. "Not so much. But your father seems rather intent these days on ensuring he makes up for the leeway he gave Robert all those years."

How interesting. "You could just fire his ass." That would be awesome.

Crew exhaled, sipped, lowered his cup. "Any other town," he said before sitting up straight, arms resting on the desk, intent blue eyes locked on me. "Seriously. But council wants a Fleming on the force and even though he's not, Robert's the closest they get to your father." There was a time I knew that would have bothered Crew, but any animosity or resentment seemed long gone, leaving good humor and a bit of frustration behind. "So, he stays, and I get to watch your father teach him a few lessons."

I grinned. "Fair enough."

Crew's right hand slid forward, grasping mine gently, fingers tucking under my palm, thumb stroking over the back. I shivered at the unexpected delicate tenderness of his touch, my own fingers reflexively closing over his tanned skin.

"How are things at the annex?" Was that further roughness in his voice? Longing in his eyes to match mine? I really needed to get him out of the office so I could kiss him again. Opportunities to kiss Crew were few and far between, the kind of adventure that really needed to take priority.

I blinked as I realized I hadn't answered him in far longer than was appropriate. His grin and sparkling eyes told me he knew exactly what I was thinking about.

Down. Girl. *Phew.*

"Jared, Alicia and I did the final walkthrough just a little while ago," I said, leaning back, freeing my hand though it was the last thing I wanted to do. But if I was going to be coherent and able to talk and adult and behave, he couldn't touch me like that. Since when was hand holding so amazingly attractive?

Fiona Fleming. Deep breaths.

Crew sat back again. "You'll have to give me a tour." Um, wow, smoldering suggestiveness was his forte this afternoon. Because that was totally an invitation for some up close and personal interaction, and he was going to get a swift kick under his desk if he didn't smarten up because hormones? Check. Brink of breaking his no kissing in his office rule? Check.

Naughty thoughts out of control? You betcha.

I had to change the subject before this turned into something I'd blush over later. "Jared invited me to the zip line park opening tomorrow." I had lost none of my blurtiness, thank you very much, but at least I was trying to be a good girl.

Crew's face tightened, his flirting subsiding as he sighed. "I know he's your friend—"

"Don't even try to stop me from going," I said. That was better. A bit of temper did wonders to burn off my need to slip into his lap and find out firsthand if he tasted like the coffee he was drinking.

He flashed me a smile and a long-suffering eye roll. "I would never," he said. "I know better. It's just…" Crew paused, setting down his coffee, hands folding together. "I'm expecting a crowd, Fee. There are protestors arriving from all over the state." He scowled briefly, gaze out the window into the sunshine, darkening his handsome face. "Olivia wants me to keep it quiet, but there's media coming, too. She won't let me call the state police in, so I'm hoping I'll have enough bodies to prevent anything serious from happening." He met my eyes again, a small, wicked smile on his face. "Knowing you'll be there? Yeah, there's bound to be trouble."

Smartass sheriff. "Ha. Ha, ha. You're hilarious." And adorably edible. Sigh.

Crew reached for his coffee again. "Just, do me a favor," he said. "No dead bodies, okay?"

He'd pay for that. I arched an eyebrow while I considered what he said prior to being a smartypants. Alicia mentioned a protest, but seriously? "It can't be that bad," I said.

Crew finished his coffee, tossing it with expert

aim into the trash. "I've worked a lot of protests," he said. "They can get pretty ugly, Fee. Just be careful, okay?" That was real concern on his face now. "Promise?"

I murmured the appropriate platitude while I finished my own coffee, privately scoffing at his concern. This wasn't California, after all. This was Reading, Vermont, the cutest town in America. How bad could it possibly get?

CHAPTER SIX

Shocked, who me? As I pulled into the parking lot of *Zip It!*, the bright, cheery sign depicting a cartoon family happily suspended over a painted tree line backdrop, it was increasingly apparent my estimation of what to expect from the protest was a far cry from reality. The small army of angry people of varying ages and ethnicities brandished large signs on stakes held in both hands, shaking the various slogans etched in large, black letters at the narrow line of white-painted sawhorses holding them back from the entry to the park. My hands clenched on the steering wheel a moment, stomach knotting and honestly, if it hadn't been Jared who'd asked, I might have turned around there and then. But the sight of his Wilkins Construction truck parked near the front gate—flanked by two deputy cruisers and Crew's own sheriff's 4X4—was enough of a reminder I wasn't here for me.

I parked as far from the crowd as I could get, tucking my little car in behind a pair of SUVs, foreign plates telling me I'd likely just chosen the worst possible spot. It didn't look like there were any tourists here after all. And none of the faces in the crowd seemed familiar.

No, that wasn't true. As I tugged at the hem of my fitted t-shirt, acutely aware how tight my black capris were considering I was about to march past a line of people who would likely be judging me the entire time, I recognized a handful of the rumbling group. In fact, two of them were staying at Petunia's, the older man and his companion from the afternoon before prominent in the front of the line, their floppy hats and khaki vests now irritatingly trite. Yikes, I'd been housing opponents of Jared's park at my place? I wish I'd known. Solidarity won over discomfort, and I was already planning to give them the boot as I squared my shoulders and strode for the gate, head high.

Let them look at my butt. I wasn't dressed like this for them.

Okay, so my confidence flagged a bit as I realized the two vans near Jared's truck had major network news logos on the side and that the large, bulky cameras panning the crowd might track over me any second now. My plan to catch Crew's eye in this particular outfit—seriously, Fee, when did you devolve to sixteen again?—knowing he'd be here this morning was acutely out of synch with reality. Like that was a shocker. At least I'd been running again on a regular basis, so my darling of a jerk cousin Robert couldn't say anything negative about the size of my rear end.

Well, he could try. From the scowl on his face as I slowed my approach, he wasn't happy to see me there. That put the clip back in my step, enough to carry me past the two reporters talking into their network cameras without stumbling and making a fool of myself.

Go me. Awkwardness avoided. So far.

A twinge of regret won through my renewed confidence as I caught sight of the empty front gate and lack of locals showing the kind of support I'd hoped to see. Come to think of it, the parking lot, while rather full, felt more like outsider recrimination than Reading townsfolk come to show their love for this new venture. My heart went out to Jared and his friends, cutting out the rest of my nervousness, and I actually found I was angry as I crossed from the parking lot blacktop onto the wide gravel path leading to the front entry.

Right past the protestors. Nice of them to start yelling at me, wasn't it? And waving their ridiculous signs, "Woodpeckers are People Too" and "Save the Red Cockaded" and "Bird Murderers" like I was their mortal enemy. While I was as environmentally conscious as the next girl, this kind of uber-vegan, tree-hugging, wannabe mass-market posing in the guise of doing good for the planet made my stomach turn. Maybe if they weren't all dressed like hipster lumberjacks in their designer plaid and $200 leather boots, I'd be more willing to accept that the crowd shouting over one another so loudly I couldn't make out individual voices might actually mean what they said.

Cynical, you betcha.

No way was I giving them attention, though it was apparent from the grim nod Jill gave me, the frustrated redness of Robert's cheeks, they'd had it about up to their gun holsters with the rabid pack already. Crew would be missing the state police today and likely cursing out Olivia for not allowing him to call in backup.

Frankly, I didn't wish this job on anyone, not even my irritating cousin.

"WHERE ARE YOU GOING, YOUNG WOMAN?"

I screamed. I couldn't help myself. The augmented blast in my right ear made me jump almost out of my skin as I leaped to one side, both hands clutching at my chest, air torn from my lungs while I spun with goosebumps racing over my bare arms. The man with the offending bullhorn met my gaze, the soon-to-be former guest of Petunia's jutting out his narrow chest under that ridiculous multi-pocketed vest of his. Hazel eyes burned with the kind of zealot crazy that looked more like obsession than passion for a cause. He grinned at me, nasty, twisting before bellowing into the bullhorn again. "ARE YOU A MURDERER?"

The crowd started chanting, right on cue. "Murderer, murderer, murderer," the man turning to face them, still shouting into his mouthpiece. "Murderer, murderer, murderer!"

To be fair, I hated being scared, loathed it. Thanks to Robert, of all people. Instead of running when I was startled, I tended to strike out instead. Enough years of my cousin's gleeful attempts to make me scream had created a kind of perfect storm that blurred the lines between fear and hang on while I punch you in the face. Now, normally I was able to control it, especially as a grown woman. I wasn't a teenager anymore, and it had been a long time since anyone purposely scared me like that.

Maybe that was the problem? Whatever the case, as the older man turned away, stirring up his eager followers, floppy hat triggering my rage for no reason whatsoever, my ears still ringing from the assault of his attack, something inside me literally snapped in half. Heat rose in waves from my stomach, washing outward in a rush of magma, flooding my vision with the kind of red haze I'd heard about and always scoffed at as make-believe.

It would have ended badly. With me under arrest, likely with blood on my hands, shrieking like a wild woman and frothing at the mouth with the horrid man's body crushed to the ground beneath me. I have utter confidence that had I managed to take that one fateful step my feet begged me to stride, neither Jill nor Robert would have been able to keep me from flinging myself bodily into the crowd.

Instead, in the exact moment the heat wave in the core of me broke, a touch settled on my elbow, and someone took their life into their own hands, firmly leading me forward and away. My head snapped around, fists clenching at my sides, ready to fight, only to look up into worried brown eyes and a faint, fearful smile on a ruggedly handsome face.

Not the eyes I was expecting, to be honest, nor the body attached to them. My anger shifted to startled acquiescence in a heartbeat, almost staggering me. Had it been Crew on the other end of that guiding hand things might actually have been worse. I'd spent enough time fighting him in the past over behaving myself, after all, and despite our recent happier interactions, there was enough history I'm pretty sure he'd have heard an earful I'd have regretted later.

Instead, I found myself walking quickly along beside Ranger Matt Winston, his hat pulled down over his brow, long legs in dark green park uniform pants and khaki shirt tight over his broad chest. "This way, Fee," he said, tenor voice just loud enough to reach me past the shouting protestors, almost directly in my ear. I shivered from the touch of his breath, more so though from the abrupt shift in emotion as he guided me through the main gate and into the park on the other side.

"This is ridiculous," I snapped, finally getting a hold of myself again, tugging my arm from his hand. I spun and glared at the protestors, refraining from offering their leader my middle finger in response to his continuing attention. Far too gleeful in his personal attack of my person, if you asked me. "Didn't the Fish and Wildlife Service clear the park?"

Matt's earnest face seemed more boyish than ever. I'd known him since elementary school and always liked him, though we hadn't really reconnected since I came home. Sure, I'd seen him at Sammy's, run into him a time or to. But I'd been so busy I honestly hadn't even thought about him past the occasional encounter. "They did," he said, keeping his voice low, hands on his narrow hips. "And as far as I know that's not been rescinded. Trouble is, these people have the right to protest all they want as long as they don't break the law."

Grumble, mumble. I struggled to pull my temper under control, the urge to march back through the gate and confront the jerk with the bullhorn with his short, roundness and balding head and his idiotic multi-pocket vest and jeans tucked into his rubber boots just feeding the overwhelm of emotion. The second I cooled off enough not to yell at Daisy I was kicking his ass out of my bed and breakfast and banning him for life.

So there.

"Olivia and the council aren't happy." Matt sounded almost mournful. How much of the brunt was he carrying, considering his job as park ranger for the area? "I hate to say it, but I think this place might fail before it has a chance to even get started. No one wants to come." He flashed me a quick grin, white teeth bright against his tanned skin. "Except you, Fee. You were always braver than the average girl."

I wasn't so sure brave was the right word, but whatever. "Poor Jared," I said.

Matt didn't get to respond. When he drew a breath to speak, as if by some predetermined signal, the crowd of protestors surged forward, pushing against Jill and Robert, and, with his bullhorn waving and leading the way, their arrogant ass of an instigator came charging toward us.

CHAPTER SEVEN

Spoiling for a fight, who, me? While I might have been less likely to choke the living crap out of the arrogant snot with the bullhorn from hell, the surge of adrenaline he'd created—and the burgeoning can of whoop-ass he'd cracked open with his little shouty stunt—still raced through my veins and not even Matt's gentle attempt to stop me could keep my Fleming redheaded temper in check this time.

The group stopped just short of trespassing, toeing the line at the gate while I leaned into it, dodging the bullhorn as the man lowered it and flashed me another nasty grin.

"You didn't answer my question," he said in an oddly mild voice that surprised me enough I froze a moment.

"You're supporting the deaths of innocent

woodpeckers not seen in this region for years." The older woman next to him spoke up next, brown eyes bulging, her squat body squashed into her own matching version of environmentalist mountain store chic. One of her big, square boots stubbed against the toe of my sneaker, the steel reinforcement sending a zing of pain up my leg. I was high enough on my temper to ignore it while she practically spat in my face, her graying hair pulled into a severe bun that tugged at the lines around her eyes. "Murderer!"

I caught Jill's struggle to reach me out of the corner of my eye, but I had this covered. Especially since it seemed like the protesters were all talk and no actual action outside their pretense at breaking the line in the gravel. "So, show me a woodpecker," I said.

I don't think the leader was expecting that. In fact, I was a little surprised by my own restraint. While his hazel eyes flickered with annoyance, his crowd of earth-mother hungry followers frothing to comply with his every desire, I realized just how coldly calculated he was, saw it written in the flare of irritation he shared before I grinned in his face.

"Well?" I looked over the line of protestors, back to him. He was slightly shorter than me, though my 5'7" could hardly be called towering, but it was enough of a difference when I stood straighter, I could almost see over his head. Being a barista and a waitress for years taught me to stand up for myself without actually insulting the customer, though the past little while running Petunia's had given me more of an edge knowing it was my place without a boss to tell me to smile and let the guy buying coffee treat me like crap if he felt like it. I felt a rather hysterical giggle building in my chest, fed by the truth I was about to have some fun despite the continuing bubble of anger I rode. "Show me one of the cute little fellas and I'm outta here."

"Lewis," the woman snapped in his ear.

"Hang on a moment, Grace," he said, lowering his bullhorn further, waving at the people crowding behind him while light panned over us from the cameras hovering past Jill's shoulder. Great, I was on television. Awesome. Just what I needed. But no way was I backing down from this artificial and contrived little crap disturber. "Our fair hostess has a point." Lovely, he knew who I was. "The problem is, young lady, we've been denied access to the site in question. Which means I can't comply with your request, can I?"

"So, this whole show and tell is lacking in show," I shot back. Let the cameras roll on that truth. "Speculation to make a mess. Nice job."

The woman he'd called Grace grimaced. "We have it on good authority," she grumbled. "No red cockaded woodpeckers have been seen in this area in well over fifty years. But a live specimen was spotted and despite our efforts to expose the cover-up of local government," way to stir the crowd again, lady, "we've been cut off from proving those precious little lives are at risk!"

Dear god, enough with the rhetoric. Though,

clearly, it was enough to set off the group again and while I stood there, Matt hovering at my side, my chest tight from the need to laugh and scream at the same time, I realized it didn't matter. The truth was irrelevant. And I was wasting my breath.

I turned toward the ranger beside me to toss my hands and give up when I spotted a small cluster of people heading our way from the low, square building that had to be the main office. Jared looked about as grim as I'd ever seen him, even more so than the night he'd caught me red-handed in his father's office shortly after Pete was murdered. And the tall, handsome sheriff at his side wasn't much happier. Yeah, I'd be hearing about my lack of self-control in detail if the tick under Crew's left eye was any indication. The other two who joined them in their approach were strangers to me, though Alicia's mention of Carmen and Aiden had to be identifiers. They wore matching *Zip It!* t-shirts and looked anxious enough about the gathering they approached—the handsome young man with the blond hair and lean build worried and the young woman with the dark hair in an aggressively swinging ponytail—about as pissed as I was if I read them right.

I backed off, shaking myself internally, knowing I'd get nowhere from here and wishing I'd kept my temper instead of challenging Lewis. Stupid and probably unhelpful and had done nothing to eliminate my need to do physical harm to his smirking face.

Temper, Fee. Sheesh.

Matt tried to guide me by my elbow again—like he knew I needed the help to stay out of trouble— but I refused to let him make contact, striding to join Jared who stopped in front of me with his eyes on the crowd and his jaw jumping.

"Thanks for coming," he said, not once meeting my gaze. "Sorry to drag you into this. It's way worse than I thought."

He did not get to feel guilty. "This is stupid," I snapped, turning on Crew who squinted at me with those blue eyes like he knew I was going to ask something of him he couldn't follow through on. "How can they get away with this? They have zero proof of anything, but they can just slander the crap out of a local business and no one can stop them?"

I knew one thing for certain. If this had been Petunia's? Hell would be paid in the blood of my enemies. Snarl.

Instead of answering, Crew looked away. I did my best not to shout coward at him in my head while Jared sagged slightly, finally meeting my eyes while his two friends crowded close, the girl with her arms crossed over her chest.

"This was a terrible idea," my young, hard-working and awesome friend said.

Oh *hell* no.

I turned to find Matt had left me, joined Jill and Robert in an attempt to move the protesters back away from the gate again. I found myself toe-to-toe with Crew, hating that I had to ask the next tough questions.

"When are you going to call the state police?" He needed help, didn't he, Olivia or no Olivia? This had to end.

When he met my eyes, his were so tight I could barely see blue past his slitted lids. "I was told," he said in a voice so cold I was surprised I didn't see a puff of condensation pass his lips, "to leave them out of it." Wow. And he listened? I knew he'd felt his position was uneasy before now, but was he worried about his job so much he would risk someone getting hurt to keep it? "For now, the protestors have stayed outside the park. For now." He looked down at me again. "I'm monitoring the situation." Nodded.

Okay. So, he'd make the call if need be and, from the tension in him he wasn't happy about holding back. Trouble was, if he had to make that call, it would likely be too late.

"Lewis Brown has a huge following," Jared said, "and his right hand, Grace Perkins, is no less known. They both have a history of conflict. Bringing in more muscle just makes them double down." He shrugged, glanced at Crew like he wished he could undo every decision he'd made about the park up to now. "The mayor and council figured it would be best to just let this protest run its course."

Oh, fantastically brilliant and the idiotic idea of the century. "Olivia can't be serious."

Crew's chill snapped as he answered. "I'm not so sure anymore it was up to her."

What was that look he fixed me with? And was all

that bubbling anger aimed at me? Or was I just in the way of it for the moment?

"What do you want us to do, Crew?" I hated the sound of defeat in Jared's voice. "I never meant for this to go so wrong." He ran one hand over his face while his two friends wavered next to him, both silent and expectant while the sheriff twitched just a bit, jaw grinding a moment.

"This isn't your fault, Jared," Crew said, voice low-pitched and without the kind of gravelly anger I was expecting. "I'm sick of it, but my hands are tied." He actually looked briefly heartbroken, long enough I knew his expression earlier had nothing to do with me. I almost reached for him in a flare of empathy for what this damned job was putting him through, discarding my judgment and wishing I could help. Instead, I held back. He didn't need my sympathy out in the open like this. He needed authority and I couldn't give him that. "Unless they take action that breaks the law, they can stay."

"Both Lewis and Grace are linked to violence," Jared said. "We knew as soon as they trolled the forums and caught wind of a chance at national press this might take a nosedive. The last thing I want is that kind of negative attention for Reading."

He hardly had the corner market on negative press. There'd been enough murders in our little town over the last two years surely a few endangered and likely fictional woodpeckers weren't going to make things much less appealing to the throngs of tourists who flooded our town.

Then again, maybe I was wrong this time. Dead football heroes and fake psychics didn't have the kind of impact on people as the plight of innocent creatures threatened by man. While it was likely just a racket for attention, it was an effective one.

Crew's concern was real enough, though when he spoke, he sounded like he'd been practicing what he had to say. "No one's been able to prove wrongdoing, Jared."

Proof, right. That was kind of necessary. Though how could they continue to thrive while this park might not all on the basis of the same lack of evidence? No proof of criminal behavior and no proof of woodpeckers.

Jared shook his head like he was making up his mind about something. "There's been enough fires lit and vandalism and physical attacks when they show up to protest this can only go one way." He hesitated, glanced sideways at his friends. "Guys, I'm so sorry. But we have no choice, here. We have to shut this down."

CHAPTER EIGHT

Before I could argue with him, Jared's female friend spoke up, the bitterness in her voice enough to cut through the haze of my lingering anger.

"This is going to ruin us." She didn't sound like she held it against Jared, at least, but the glare she shot at the gathering of protestors made me worry for their physical safety. Considering what I'd been thinking myself I needed to stop being a hypocrite.

"We'll have a new assessment done," Crew said, his tone clearly appeasing, though the gruffness of his voice told me he was about as happy as they were. Still no animosity aimed in my direction? Score. "Things will settle down and you can get back to business."

"We're so low on capital I'm not sure we're able to hold off." The young man's earnest face had settled into the kind of glum acceptance that made me want to shake him. Quitting already? Not on my watch. "Besides, even if we are cleared it'll take weeks to get the assessment done and by then the one-star reviews will bury us."

I knew a thing or two about reviews and snorted despite myself. "Trust me," I said, "this is Reading. It seems like the worse the press the more people want to visit." Threatened woodpeckers or not, people were so weird.

The young woman scrunched her nose at me, her disbelief tinged in irritation. "We'll see. If we get the chance." She glanced up at Jared with an eyebrow raise while my young friend smacked himself in the forehead.

"Sorry, guys," he said, "my bad. Fiona Fleming, this is Carmen Martinez," she nodded to me, dark eyes weighing me as if judging my worth, "and Aiden Jackson. Carmen, Aiden, Fee Fleming."

I shook their hands as the dark-haired girl relented a bit, despite the continuing chanting from the peanut gallery. Funny, I was getting used to the noise of their constant chatter, so much so I was tuning them out. Perfect.

"Nice to meet you," I said.

"Fee owns the B&B I was telling you about," Jared said, perking just a little. He squeezed my shoulder and the pair seemed to relax the rest of the way, their friend's vetting clearly good enough for them.

"Sorry about the mess," Aiden said, his light

tenor peaking as he shrugged. "Thanks for coming."

"Yeah," Carmen said, a faint smile rising before she crossed her arms again, staring at the crowd. "Nice of you to show your support." She didn't sound like she meant it.

"Carmen." Aiden sighed, one arm going around her shoulders from behind, pulling her to him. So, they were a couple? Looked that way, though she resisted him at first. "We'll figure it out."

"Let me front you some more capital," Jared said, face strained. "I'm sure we can ride this out."

While I might not have intimate knowledge of his business, I did know Jared was working on a large number of expensive projects, from a mall development on the edge of town to an expansion at the White Valley Ski Lodge just to name two. I wondered, if Alicia was here, would she be tromping on his foot to shut him up or was he really prepared to ride this sinking ship to the bottom of the ocean?

Carmen spun on Jared, shedding Aiden's arms, hugging him quickly, her expression altering completely from angry sullenness to a surge of regret. "You've been awesome, Jay," she said, voice muffled in the front of his t-shirt. Hmmm. Did they have history I didn't know about? She seemed pretty comfortable embracing him like that. None of my business, but still made me prickle a little for Alicia's sake. Not that Jared would stray, and Carmen had Aiden, but still.

Fiona Fleming. Stop that right now.

Jared hugged her back before letting her go. She

altogether frustrating. Still, if there was a chance…

"Maybe you *can* ride it out?" Surely it couldn't last forever, past the next thing this group of noisemakers decided was worthy of their attention. "This will blow over as soon as this bunch gets tired and goes home."

"I'm not so sure," Carmen said, biting her lower lip. Movement caught my eye and I looked away as she finished, the line of cars gliding to a halt at the entrance heralding new visitors. "And I don't know that we even want to find out."

I should have offered comfort, but instead I groaned inwardly at the sight of Olivia Walker climbing out of the back of the lead town car, her face a dark mask, knowing from the determination in her padded shoulders and the peaked pink on her high cheekbones she planned to proceed whether Jared and his friends liked it or not.

CHAPTER NINE

Olivia wasn't alone, the other cars disgorging a collection of two suited men and three primly dressed women. I knew most of them by sight, of course, but I'd never really had much to do with the collected council before, at least not en masse like this. I'd refused to attend town meetings, mostly out of the need to avoid being pointed at and whispered about, though honestly, I was really too busy to go. At least, that was my best excuse.

Seeing them all gathered together like that gave me a flash of goosebumps, though I wasn't sure why. Until it hit me—Crew had mentioned back in January how his job seemed to be under threat thanks to me, something I'd pondered only a few minutes ago. He'd added that he'd felt all along the council and Reading as a whole had my back and not his. While

I'd never understood the reference, seeing the council coming toward me past the line of protestors felt like some kind of confrontation I wasn't prepared for. I found myself turning, stepping away from Jared and taking a stand beside Crew. If he noticed the shift in my position he didn't comment, as quietly watchful and grim as before while Olivia brushed past the entrance and stomped toward us, a forced smile on her angry face.

"Where is everyone?" She didn't look around. Clearly, she understood this opening was devolving into a disaster, one she likely couldn't afford if the judging and unhappy expressions worn by the bulk of her companions was any indication.

"We need to shut down the Reading opening," Jared said, firm but with regret. "I'm sorry, Olivia. It's just not safe."

Like he had anything to be sorry for. Her jaw jumped, her dark bob shining in the sunlight as she shook her head in response, smile now a snarl that she seemed desperate to keep plastered on her face even if it killed her. Just what we needed, another dead body.

"The opening," she growled, "goes ahead," she twitched faintly, "as planned."

Okay then.

I glanced over her shoulder, met familiar dark eyes. Terri Jacobs, the owner of Jacobs Flowers, nodded to me, looking distinctly uncomfortable as she rubbed one slender upper arm with her opposite hand, glancing around as if expecting to take a bullet in the back from the protestors now shouting louder than before. I liked Terri, didn't realize she'd joined the council after divorcing her gambling husband, Simon, their flower shop firmly in her possession. Her lack of enthusiasm when she was mostly a pretty happy person in general didn't bode well for the remainder of the council's attitudes about today's debacle.

"Just admit this was a terrible idea, Olivia." Oliver Watters grunted at me, a small wave all the acknowledgement I got from him, though the gruff historian and antique dealer held no animosity toward me. I wondered how his grandson, Denver Hatch, and that young inventor's psychic debunker girlfriend, Alice Moore, were getting along. I hadn't seen either of them in a couple of months and really needed to invite them for dinner at Petunia's.

The mayor twitched again, faint but enough to shiver her glossy bob. "We're going ahead," she snapped. "This is a worthy project that will mean more revenue and tourism—"

"Save the rhetoric for town meetings." I didn't know the tall, attractive man who lingered at the periphery of the council, his expensive suit and shiny leather shoes making me wonder who he might be. I thought I knew everyone in town. A newcomer to Reading looking to make a mark here, perhaps? "Just admit your little initiative is a waste of our time and effort, Olivia. Much as the disaster that was your Captain Reading embarrassment." Yikes, not something I'd be brave enough to bring up. With the debunking of the Reading hoard and the continuing ridicule aimed at the giant statue of the said captain dominating the square in our town center, that whole attempt to stir tourist interest still made me cringe. So, I could only imagine what kind of internal fireworks Olivia hid from the rest of us at his prodding her acutely visible failure to deliver on that project.

Her temper showed, though, as she spun on him, though she didn't get to argue. Instead, the slender, elderly woman beside him reached out with one tiny hand and smacked him firmly on the arm, her wrinkled apple face pursed in irritation.

"Oh, do hush, Geoffrey," Mary Claire Ambrose said, piping voice crisp despite her age. "I'm getting very tired of hearing you talk. Hello, Fiona dear." The owner of Ambrosia's Tea Room wiggled her fingers at me. "Delightful to see someone in Reading supporting this handsome young man." She winked at Jared who grinned back.

The suit she'd named Geoffrey scowled but held his tongue, though when his pale blue gaze swept over me, I had the sensation of being in the sights of a shark smelling chum in the water. Charming.

"We all want to support Jared in his efforts." The slightly plump and usually enthusiastic Sophia Bell, owner of The Bride Boudoir, looked about as happy to be at the park as Terri, though whether out of concern for her expensive heels—she kept mincing on her toes to keep the stilettos from driving into the dirt—or the audio assault from the crowd I didn't know and didn't care. "But until this matter is settled, we're only asking for trouble."

"Precisely my point," Geoffrey said, voice far too reasonable. "Perhaps after a week or so we can revisit the opening, once a new assessment is done."

"I think the damage is now irreparable," Sophia said, sniffing at the dirt on the toes of her shoes, touching delicately at her carefully sprayed updo of dark hair, speaking as if the two owners weren't standing there listening to what she said. "Regardless of the truth, this place is tainted." Her nose wrinkled faintly in disgust. "I want it noted I voted against this initiative, Olivia. I'm here under protest."

I wondered in a flash of angry impulse how much she'd protest landing on her designer ass in a mud puddle.

She turned toward Geoffrey and simpered, the direct sunlight reflecting from the powder heavily applied to her cheeks. "From an accountant's perspective," she said, "what do you think, Geoff, dear? Should we write off this mess as a failure and move on?" Clearly, she was looking for support, but would she gain enough? I opened my mouth to argue only to have Crew's hand grasp mine and squeeze.

Right. Stay out of it. Like hell.

Except, to my surprise, Geoffrey's smile returned, as greasy looking as the fresh blacktop in the parking lot.

"And ruin the hard work of these enterprising young people?" He beamed a grin at them, holding out one hand, striding forward to shake first

Carmen's then Aiden's as if he hadn't just been dissing them and the park. "Geoffrey Jenkins, accountant at large for the Patterson family. Perhaps, when this has all blown over, we can talk."

Carmen looked uncomfortable while Aiden seemed to shrink in on himself even while the name Patterson made my blood freeze over. The founding family of Reading always seemed to cling to the periphery, minding their own business from the giant manor house that loomed over Cutter Lake. I'd only really ever met Aundrea and Jared from that particular bloodline, though the demise of Mason Patterson at White Valley Ski Lodge a year and a half ago left me with a bad taste in my mouth for that particular family. The fact they were taking a distinct and visible place on town council all of a sudden?

I had to stop burying my head in dirty sheets and emails and find out what was going on. Because if they wanted Olivia out or had an agenda of their own that could lead to my detriment? I needed to know about it. Not to mention the fact if Geoffrey didn't stop staring at my chest like that I was going to make sure he couldn't add two and two ever again.

When his gaze lifted to my eyes, he tried that same smile. "Miss Fleming," he said, "the offer is open to you, too." Like I'd ever use him as an accountant. Not only did he give me the creeps, no way was I using anyone local to do my books. Best to keep my business in Reading my business, thanks.

Funny how Crew dropped my hand and took a half step forward, mostly blocking my view of the smarmy piece of work. He better not have been pulling a knight in shining armor or he'd be falling off his particular high horse in about a heartbeat. When he spoke, his normally deep and velvety voice had the kind of gravel to it more familiar from Dad and I wondered if he'd been taking John Fleming lessons in an attempt to get through to the hard heads standing before us.

"The protestors aren't going away," he said, "and a decision has to be made. My staff can handle it for now, but if this gets bigger, I'll have to call in state police."

It was clear from the instant reaction of all of the council members he'd brought this up before enough times they were tired of hearing it. Their instant rejection made my teeth ache.

"No state interference," Olivia snapped. "If you can't do the job you're hired for, Sheriff Turner—"

She did not just say that out loud. "Excuse me," I cut her off, stepping around him this time, knowing it might look like I was defending him (okay, I was) and that he might not appreciate me doing so (likely would yell at me later) but I didn't care in that moment because this was ridiculous and the answer about as obvious as the faint smirk on Geoffrey's face. He actually seemed to be enjoying himself. Why was that I wondered? Didn't matter as I pushed on, Olivia glaring at me while I turned to Carmen and Aiden. "The protestors are here because of a sighting of the woodpecker, right?" They nodded. "But no one has any proof outside some rumor there are even any here, correct?" More nodding. "Then there's one way to solve this." I gestured at the front gate. "Let them in."

Jared hissed softly, glanced at his friends, while Geoffrey's smile disappeared and Olivia looked startled, then smiled.

"An excellent idea," the mayor said, her grand and officious attitude returned in a heartbeat as she beamed at me. "Welcome the protestors inside. Show them there are no woodpeckers here. And while we're at it," she spun and waved at the gathered cameras, "we bring the media in, too. The whole world will see that *Zip It!* is home to fun and relaxation and in no way threatens the endangered species we all value and treasure."

I had no idea what the silly bird actually even looked like, but if the feathered creature was anywhere in this park, I'd eat Petunia's kibble.

CHAPTER TEN

Jared hesitated a moment longer before Crew's voice, much softer and without the harshness of before, agreed.

"It's an option," he said. "Though, again, we're thin on staff." I turned to find him squinting at the crowd, shaking his head a little. "I can't promise protection from vandalism."

"It's fine," Carmen said, lips a narrow line, "don't worry about that." She looked up at Aiden who nodded, smiling faintly. Her face brightened and she grinned at me. "Thank you, Fee. The voice of reason. It's a great idea." She turned then and strode for the protestors, Aiden scrambling to keep up, Jared joining them while I followed, Crew at my side, the council drifting after us. I caught Olivia's flash of relief, the way she wiped at her upper lip, fingertips trembling slightly and welcomed empathy for her. I even smiled when she looked up, nodded to her in solidarity and accepted the tight grin she shared in return.

Sure, Olivia Walker and I had our run-ins in the past. But there was no way I'd let her down when this park and the initiative behind it really was a great idea.

Carmen came to a halt at the gate, animosity firmly in check, her open, willing smile silencing the protest until Lewis lowered his bullhorn and waited.

"We'd like to welcome you into *Zip It!* on our opening day," she said, voice level and genuine, "to see for yourselves exactly what we've built here." She gestured at the gate, still closed, which Jared hurried toward with Aiden beside him, the two pulling the entry wide and standing back. Jill and Robert held their place, eyes on Crew, as Carmen went on. "We have nothing to hide and everything to gain in your exploration of our park."

"This is a trick." Grace glanced up at Lewis who was frowning now, his gaze never leaving the steady calm one Carmen offered. I'd never been so proud of someone in my whole life as I was of her in that moment, nor of Jared and Aiden who held their ground while the protestors looked at each other in faint shock.

Lewis finally smiled, though there was enough vitriol remaining in it I didn't doubt he'd go to great—and even fake—lengths to ensure Carmen's ruin. Surely such a confrontation out in the open like this, one that cut the legs out from under him, wasn't endearing her in any way to the blowhard. But he had two alternatives and the media were watching. Refusing her offer meant he knew she had nothing to hide. Coming into the park would prove it. Unless he had a woodpecker family up his sleeve. I wouldn't put it past him.

"We'd be delighted," he said.

"Under escort," Crew cut in, nodding to Jill and Robert who backed off, Matt appearing around the other side of the group where he'd been monitoring the side entrance to the park.

But Carmen just smiled at him. "No, Sheriff," she said, "thank you. I'm sure these fine people who love animals and nature as much as we do would never attempt to vandalize our property. They only want to know that the woodpeckers are safe." Nods and grumbling agreement and a few smiles answered her. She was winning them over, and I had to hide my own grin behind my hand. "Please, if anyone finds a nesting family, alert the authorities at once. But, if not, this park is open for business and your approval."

I'd never seen things turn around as quickly as they did then. The fifty or so protestors flooded the entrance, spreading out into the park, snapping pictures but without the kind of angry underboiling they'd been stewing in since before I arrived. I had no doubt some mischief would be sprinkled around during the day, but for now it seemed their drive to destroy had been turned into a desire to uncover the truth.

Lewis and Grace were the last through the gate, arguing quietly between them. I dodged out of the way as she bumped into me, scowling at me while one of her heavy shoes tromped on my sneakered toes. I almost pushed back, Crew her only defense while I glared after the pair, hoping there was an angry wasp nest in their future. There was little time to think past such a happy fantasy, though, not when the gathered reporters rushed the gate and tackled Carmen and Aiden. Jared himself was unable to avoid being interviewed, though I was happy at that point to have the sheriff at my side to steer me away from Olivia and the council and her politicospeach to the world, the two of us heading further into the park.

He stopped me at the edge of the main building, hand on my elbow, staring back at the reporters, the council, the young and now eager faces of the owners and spoke without looking at me, voice pitched low.

"You might have saved Olivia's job and this park with that suggestion," he said. His blue eyes met mine, but there wasn't much happiness in them. "At least, for now." He sighed, hands on his hips, head down. "Hell of an opening day."

I wasn't sure what to say. "I suppose you're going to tell me to go home now," I said.

He chuckled, a warm and delicious sound while his shoulders rounded back, a real and (oh my god) sexy smile pulling at his full mouth. The temptation to just grab him and kiss him hit me like a freight train, taking me by breathless surprise while he spoke.

"Wouldn't dream of it, Miss Fleming," he said. "Figure you're planning to follow around a few protestors and make sure they stay honest?"

He really did know me better than he should for someone who hadn't had a date with me yet. "That transparent, huh?" I was itching to find out what Lewis and Grace were up to. Because they were up to something. My Fleming sense of suspicious behavior tingled so much across the back of my neck I would shiver from it any second now.

He laughed then, shook his head, tipped his white hat. "Just be careful, please?" Crew hesitated like he wanted to say more but stiffened and straightened, humor vanishing as his face went tight. I turned to find Olivia approaching at a clip and when I glanced back to tell Crew I would watch my step he was striding away, joining Jill and Robert, Matt waiting with them.

When I spun to face Olivia again, she didn't seem to notice her own sheriff didn't want to talk to her and my compassion for her position died the fastest death any emotion ever suffered in the history of feelings. My temper snap-crackled but didn't get to emerge, not when the mayor grasped my elbow much as Crew had, her expression forced smiling again but her dark eyes full of anger.

"At least someone has my back around here," she said, voice pitched low. "Thank you for being here, Fee, for being loyal to your town. I can always count on you and your parents to have Reading's best interests at heart." Hmmm. Where did that come from? Dad had been a popular sheriff, but I wasn't exactly well-loved, considering I'd been present for a number of untimely deaths since I got home. "I do wish I could convince you to run for council. I could use your voice. Or your mother's, for that matter."

Whoa, what? This was the first I'd heard of any such desire on her part and sat so far outside my radar I couldn't muster a reply due to sheer shock. At least on my part. As for Mom and Dad? Maybe Olivia didn't realize Mom wasn't herself since that stupid show in January. I opened my mouth to let her have it after all, regaining control—loosely termed—of my tongue and temper when the mayor rushed on as if she had no idea, not one inkling, of the truth of the devastation she'd left behind her with that horrible choice.

"No matter and you don't have to decide now. But I do know you understand just how important the continuing efforts of my position are in supporting and growing the tourism industry in Reading. This place doesn't sell itself." She wiped at her upper lip again, though whether from stress or from the heat of the day troubling her in her full suit I wasn't sure. "The council seems to think that the efforts I've made up until now are sufficient." Was that faint panic in her eyes? "They have no idea the kind of continuing pressure that needs to be applied, the marketing and strategies that placing Reading's name and brand in the hearts and minds of tourists requires." I guess I didn't either, then. Was I taking it all for granted? "You are the only one who appreciates just how much money and commitment goes into maintaining brand recognition, let alone stimulating growth." She gave me too much credit. I was winging it, for the most part, felt myself flush with the desire to deny her compliment. "Well, you and Vivian. We really must sit down together and look at my vision. I'd love your input into direction next quarter."

Whoa, she'd what? "Um, okay." Fee, shut up, for goodness's sake. Agree to nothing. Nothing.

But that was the right response, apparently. Olivia beamed at me before her face darkened once again. "I am acutely aware of who it was sabotaged this park and my recent efforts to publicize the Reading hoard and our famous ancestor." She didn't turn around, glaring her fury at me instead like I was the perpetrator. "And I'm taking steps to eliminate the threat." Yikes, this was small-town politics, not an arms race. Then again, there was a lot of money at stake, wasn't there? My own business was proof of that. "Your continued support is greatly appreciated." She let me go and I rubbed at my elbow, sure I'd have bruises there in the morning. "Say hello to your parents for me, won't you?" And, with that, she spun and left, waving for the cameras and getting into her car, her council following while the media continued their barrage at the young owners of the park and my mind churned.

A traitor on council. I could guess. But why were

the Pattersons suddenly so interested in politics? I briefly considered trying to talk to Geoffrey Jenkins but held my place as he climbed into the back of one of the cars, accepting the excuse he was already leaving, and I could go question him later about his and the family's motives. Never mind the idea of actually having a conversation with him made me want to take a shower. A long, boiling shower with bleach.

Instead, chest tight with the need to do something, no matter what that something might be, I decided playing snoop here at the park was the happier alternative. Seeing Carmen and Aiden—and Jared—win against the protest would be most satisfying.

That was, as long as no one found a woodpecker. Better not. I was looking forward to a victory.

CHAPTER ELEVEN

By the time Carmen, reporters in tow, smiled at me from behind the counter of the welcome center most of the lingering unhappiness that had plagued my arrival was gone. Instead, her smile and the growing enthusiasm of Aiden and Jared fed my own grin as I stepped up, the first paying guest of *Zip It!*

"ID, please," she said. "We need a scan for insurance purposes."

I gaped at her. "You're kidding." I'd naturally left it in the car. But after all this surely, she'd let it slide?

Nope, not happening, and I guess I didn't blame her. She firmly shook her head, addressing the cameras pointed in her face. "We're strictly by the book here at *Zip It!*," she said. "Safety and protocols are of the utmost importance to keeping our visitors safe."

Grumble, mumble, fine, whatever. I did my best not to show my irritation—I'd saved her freaking park, hadn't I?—and instead headed back out into the sunny late morning and the parking lot. Felt weird to walk away with cameras at my back, that creeping feeling of being watched not helping even a little bit, though it was only because I was acutely aware of the scrutiny this entire place was under. It was almost a relief to pass through the gates and onto the blacktop, to retreat to my car and for a moment I considered just getting in and driving away. After all, Jared didn't really need me anymore. The crisis was handled, at least for now. Except, of course, my inner busybody refused to drive off without resolution and I grinned at myself as I unlocked the front door and fished my wallet out of the dash. Sometimes being nosy was a pain in the ass.

I nabbed my hoody from the back seat, tying it around my waist, not sure if I'd be needing it and kicking myself a bit for failing to use it earlier as a shield from the camera attention. Whatever. So, my rear was on national television? As I straightened, still chuckling about the vicious cycle of stay versus go I'd created for myself, I noticed movement among the cars across the divide of the parking lot. A tall, thin blonde with a camera crept through the lines of vehicles, snapping pictures of license plates. I crossed to her as quietly as I could, frowning as I noted her taking photos of even Jared's truck and when I came to a halt next to her heard her meep in surprise to be caught in the act.

She stood to her full height, a few inches above mine, her slim frame willowy, long narrow face thin and faintly tanned. Her pale brown eyes seemed guilty, but she laughed a bit at her shock and shook her head.

"You startled me," she said in a soft alto.

"Are you a journalist?" I didn't mean to sound threatening, but sneaking pictures wasn't exactly something that endeared me, considering my own car sat in this lot.

She hesitated before shrugging. "Fleur King." She offered her hand, and I shook it, surprised by the strength in her fingers despite her slender appearance.

"Fiona Fleming." I dropped her hand, crossing my arms over my chest, glancing at Jared's plate. "Finding anything interesting, Miss King?"

She grinned, swiping a strand of thick, blonde hair out of her face. "A few things," she said. "You're friends with the owners?"

An honest guess. I was about to reply, however, that wasn't exactly any of her business when I heard Crew call my name. I glanced over at the entrance, watched him head in my direction, and turned back to find Fleur had ducked away from me, waving as she vanished around the side of Jared's truck. Apparently, people walking away from me when I was distracted was going to be a thing for me today. The first person who did it to me earlier seemed to have had a change of heart, though, as the sheriff came to a halt beside me. His gaze followed mine as I turned back to where Fleur had vanished.

"Trouble?" He sounded amused by the word and the suggestion I'd found some was likely.

I almost smacked him. "Funny guy, ha ha. You should try standup."

He winked, nudging me with his elbow. "I'm here all week."

Amazing how his blue eyes could make me want to grab him and kiss him. No, not just his eyes. How many times did I have to say *down, girl* before it stuck?

"I was thinking," he said, "things are under control, at least for now." He cleared his throat, looked down at the ground, then up at me again. "I want to stick around, and I know you're staying put. There might be a great way to keep an eye on this place where we can both snoop."

This was sounding interesting. "You up for some zip-lining, Sheriff Turner?"

He grinned suddenly, boyishly, pushing one big hand through his dark hair. "I haven't done it in a while, and I love it." He sobered before smiling again like he fought the compulsion. "I'm still working, but Jared suggested it. It's a great idea." It was clear he struggled with the mix of business and pleasure.

Well, if he was looking for me to give him permission, I was all for it. The thought of swinging through the trees like Tarzan and Jane had the instant kind of zinging appeal that made me laugh, so low and full of a burst of lusty passion it shocked me. And him, from the way his pupils dilated and his whole body swayed toward me.

"Not the first date I was hoping for," I said, leaning in to place one hand on his chest, over his heart. It was beating about as fast as mine all of a sudden. "But I'll take it."

Crew's answering grin had far more heat in it than even the sun overhead. And as we crossed together to the entry of the park, I wondered suddenly what it would be like to kiss him suspended at thirty feet.

I can honestly say I've never had that much fun in my entire life. While I was expecting to enjoy myself, the following hours spend flying through the treetops with Crew at my side bordered on the type of hilarious joy that brought me back to childhood abandon. A quick call to Daisy while the sheriff hovered, waiting for me to hurry up already, devolved into whispering giggles as she encouraged me to take my time. Guilt washed clear the moment he took my hand and I followed him with the kind of skipping delight I knew I'd be embarrassed to look back on later.

As it turned out, stealing the occasional kiss from him on the towering platforms just before flying away on a thin line in a rush of air while laughing breathlessly over the sensation of his mouth on mine offered the sort of giddy rush that I hadn't expected from today or any day. And, as we continued to explore the park, navigating the high ropes and the purposely rickety bridges of disconnected boards, climbing and gliding and embracing in the shadowing leaves for instants of private passion, I felt this giant bubble of happiness build and build inside me until I was positive I would never come down from the high that was Crew Turner.

My plan to keep an eye on the protestors evaporated every time he hooked one arm around my waist and tucked me against him, the pair of us lost for a moment in each other's gaze. More often than not he would kiss me first, though I claimed my fair share of delicious encounters before pushing off and leaving him behind to follow.

He, at least, held onto a shred of responsibility, calling in on occasion to check with Jill and Robert on the state of the hunt for the endangered birds. Aside from the theft of some rope from the entrance building that Aiden seemed to think was a big deal, nothing untoward broke through our fun. As the afternoon began to age and the mostly satisfied protesters began to exit the park empty-handed, a sense of peace and delight devoured my worry and, it seemed, lulled Crew out of the kind of tense observation that felt most common in him.

We only encountered one real issue as the day wore on. As I touched down at the bottom of a hand-over-hand bridge, the lines over my head and wiggling rope under my feet knocking me off balance, I stumbled and caught myself as someone barreled past, sign swinging beside him. It hooked the edge of my harness just as I disconnected from the line, spinning me sideways and pushing my already wobbly self into a hard fall on my butt. I woofed out some air in a grumbling complaint, Crew landing gracefully next to me in time to grasp the arm of the young man who'd knocked me over.

"Careful," the sheriff growled. "Watch where you're going."

The young man tried to shake free before noticing the badge on Crew's shirt, his characteristic white had gone in favor of the helmet Carmen fitted him with. Irritation turned to surprise as my unwitting assailant finally seeming to realize who he was talking to.

"Sorry," he said, not meaning it, though he did meet my eyes with his own pale green ones as I pulled myself to my feet, brushing dirt from my backside and trying not to blush from the clumsy fall.

"Name," Crew snapped.

"Philip Davis," he said, turning to me again, this time with what looked like regret, boots grinding into the dirt as he spun in my direction. "I am sorry, miss."

I shrugged it off. "Did you have any luck finding the woodpeckers?" I didn't mean to sound sarcastic. Oh, wait, yeah, I did. Sue me.

How lovely for him to look so distinctly uncomfortable, glancing back over his shoulder, his expression guilty. Trying to plant some evidence, young man? "Not yet," he said. Crew let him go and he nodded to both of us before hurrying off again.

Crew looked like he wanted to go after him, almost did. His momentum was cut off before it began, stopped by Carmen who appeared out of nowhere from the direction Philip had just stormed from. She stumbled to a halt, staring at us like she wasn't expecting us to be there.

"Everything okay?" My handsome sheriff—yes, mine, back off Captain Gorgeouspants and you won't get hurt—showed his typical concern, but she just shook her head, forced a smile.

"Protestors," she said. "Just keeping an eye on them."

Hmmm. This from the woman who told him not to bother? "Good so far?"

She nodded then, looked relieved. "Having fun?"

I grinned, couldn't help it. "You're getting a great review from me," I said.

Carmen left us, waving, pursuing the disappearing figure of Philip Davis, leaving Crew to stare after her with his trademark frown. I took a chance and cupped his face in one hand, turning him toward me. Reached up on tiptoe to kiss the end of his nose. Winked.

Crew laughed. And followed me as I raced up the next tree.

Thank goodness I'd started running again or I never would have survived an hour. It was hard work, but so much fun, and being fit again could only benefit me as the summer unfolded. I really needed to make sure I kept up with it. I wondered if Crew would be into morning jogs. Or some other form of exercise that elevated the heart rate.

Fiona Fleming. Naughty, naughty.

Maybe it was just I finally got to see the real Crew. Or I preferred to believe I was a good influence on him. Either way, as my watch hit 3PM with that final climb and my energy level began to flag, I was positive the last of his reticence had been washed away by the fun of the day. Who knew such a horrible and stressful beginning could turn out quite so delightful?

I came to a panting halt at the top of the last platform in the row, one we'd zipped several times already. It was the longest of the grouping, stretching out into the treetops, well sheltered at the beginning by a tunnel of branches and leaves that made a stunning oasis of green shadows and cool air fed by a soft breeze. The perfect day for zip-lining if I did say so myself. I turned as Crew landed next to me, so close I could feel his breath on my cheek before he bent to press his lips to my ear.

"Have dinner with me tonight." The gruffness of his voice made me shiver all over, especially when he didn't move after speaking, mouth grazing over my earlobe, faint trace of his teeth nibbling at the edge. He was lucky we were thirty feet up on a narrow platform because had we been on the ground? He'd have been at risk of a hard landing and some rather private activity that may or may not have ended in the pair of us getting arrested.

Seriously. Yum.

I met his eyes, took a long moment to stare into

them, force myself to breathe. I wanted to say yes, instantly and without reservation. Instead, I held his gaze, made him look at me, really look at me, before I kissed him as softly as I could.

"Ask me again when we're down," I whispered over his lips. "And if you're sure, I'm yours." Shiver. Not the choice of words I'd meant, but, well. Yeah.

His.

He didn't respond, waited for me to pull away. Watched as I checked my helmet and switched over my carabiner from the climb rope tethered to the platform support line to the zip line before unhooking as I'd been taught. Felt like a bit of overkill on the safety department, but I wasn't arguing. I stepped out onto the edge of the platform, staring down the expanse into the treetops, the bulk of it obscured from sight, fading from sunlight into shadow. And held my breath as I realized this plunge into the unknown—safe despite how it was made to appear to increase the thrill, I was sure—was a mirror to how I felt about Crew. As I smiled to myself, heart pounding over the connection I discovered, I made the physical choice symbolizing the one I would solidify tonight over dinner.

I chose to leap into the mysterious and a little scary and ride that line. I chose Crew.

It wasn't until I plunged into the dark tunnel of leaves halfway down the line, I realized someone else hung there, suspended ahead of me. There was nothing I could do to stop at that point, and I impacted the limp form, my momentum carrying both of us forward. My hands grappled for the figure, slowly turning around on the lines suspending him, the furthest platform rushing toward us, though without the speed I'd been expecting from my previous rides.

He completed his rotation, facing me, empty eyes staring into mine, Lewis Brown's limp, dead body pressed against me while we slid to a halt ten feet from the end, trapping me in his embrace, suspended above the forest floor.

While I exhaled. Inhaled.

And started to scream.

CHAPTER TWELVE

Okay, so it's not like this was my first dead body or anything. And I'd had a guy die on top of me, after all, so there was precedence set. Still, there had been tons of people around and while I'd been trapped under Skip Anderson briefly, the fact I was on the ground and rescue was quick to come had at least limited the physical contact to maybe a minute, tops.

Yeah, not so lucky this time, was I? Instead of a quick and easy whoopsie dead man crashing, I hung there, panting and doing my best not to throw up all over his slowly cooling corpse, his bulging eyes staring at me like this was all my fault for at least fifteen years.

Maybe ten minutes. It just felt like half my life. The only glimmer of a silver rim to this particularly uncomfortable and nightmare-inducing process was the fact Crew was there with me the whole time, his cool, calm voice never once letting me go.

I clung to the sound of it as he spoke, alternating between addressing me hanging on the line—with Lewis pressed against me despite my best attempts to keep him at arm's length—and using his cell phone to call for help. Have you ever tried to push a dead body away from you, one that has at least fifty pounds on your weight, while sharing an overburdened zip line? Talk about a lesson in desperate futility. Hideous, anxious, terrifying, nauseating, shock-inducing futility.

"Fee, I'm right here." Crew's voice had that kind of level strength I instantly focused on, and I did, latching onto the sound like it was the only thing keeping me from losing it entirely. "Stay with me, Fee. Jill, I need backup at the final line, now." No anxiety, no haste, just the steady tone of his voice, soothing, comforting while I panted my way in circles around hyperventilation while the remains of Lewis bumped me over and over again. "Fee, it's going to be okay, just hang on. I'm below you now." I looked down, breaking the dead man's stare, realizing my throat ached, that I'd likely done a number on my vocal chords. Odd how such thoughts cross the mind in moments of utter horror. "Fee, focus on me. You'll be all right, I promise. Stay with me."

His voice droned on, his blue eyes locked on mine. I barely noticed the feeling of the line releasing, the sound of other voices, only realized I was nearer the ground when he reached up with both hands and caught me. Suddenly we were surrounded by people, Jill and Robert, Matt, Jared, and I was in Crew's arms, the carabiner unhooked from the line, helmet lifted from my head, my head tucked against his shoulder as he carried me swiftly away in long strides.

The blanket Alicia settled around my shoulders felt like a hug, though I instantly missed Crew when he released me and returned to the body, the sight of Aiden manning a winch at the top of the opposite tree telling me how I'd made it to the ground. Carmen stood off to one side with Jared, Crew and his deputies huddled over the body while Matt seemed like he was about as close to puking as I'd been.

Jared joined us as Alicia's hand gently rubbed my back in small, anxious circles. I'm not sure who the activity was meant to help, me or her, but I appreciated the sentiment. Honestly, now that I no longer hung with the dead man's face within kissing distance—just ew, I mean like, ewie ew grossness *gag*—I was quickly recovering my composure to the point I felt bubbling giggles rising in my chest at the thought of telling Daisy about what happened.

Which meant I was lying to myself about the composure thing and likely still on the edge of hysterical. Whatever.

"They're shutting down the park." Jared's misery flared from personal to a wince of worry as he quickly sank to his haunches and grasped my hands, guilt in his eyes. "I'm sorry, Fee. I didn't mean..." he swallowed hard, squeezing my fingers. "They need to shut it down." He shook his head, forehead creasing, face ashen, aging him visibly while he struggled internally. "This is a disaster."

"Babe, it's not your fault." Alicia left me and her backrub to hug him around the shoulders, his superior height making it easier for her to embrace him that way. He pushed himself up, hugging her in turn, engulfing her a moment before letting her go.

"You didn't kill that protestor," I said, surprised at how level my voice sounded. "You did everything right, Jared." Cool, I wasn't going to fall apart at any second. "Stop beating yourself up, please. Whoever murdered Lewis Brown, whether their intent was to shut down the park or not, is to blame." I met his eyes, watched him relax somewhat, nodded. "Okay?"

Jared cleared his throat while Alicia gave me a brave smile, blinking tears from her lashes.

"Okay," my handsome young friend said. "Are you okay, Fee?"

I'd probably freak out with a serious case of willies later and my throat ached from screaming, but otherwise, the hysterical need to cackle like a madwoman had eased and the shaking weakness I only now realized kept me from standing up was gone from my knees and thighs. I exhaled long and slow, inhaled without a quiver, nodded again. "All good."

Matt appeared, crouched next to me, anxious expression mirrored in the tight grasp of his hands on mine. "Are you okay?" The ranger seemed distraught, and I think would have hugged me if I hadn't leaned away from him. I was just pulling myself together and another embrace would be the end of my thin bit of control.

I nodded swiftly, smiled. Pretended. Because pretending was all I could manage.

Jill hurried over, worried frown focused on me, though when she glanced at the handsome park ranger crouched at my feet something flickered across her face that made me wonder. No time to figure out what she was thinking, though, because she bent next to Matt to take my other hand, face earnest. "Everyone scattered when we came running," she said. "Toby's going to check the video feed to try to track down who was here, but it's a bit of an investigative mess." She squeezed my hand before letting me go. "Doc Aberstock will be here shortly. He'll need to examine your clothes where you, um. Had contact. With the victim." Jill glanced up at Jared and Alicia. "We should probably just take them if that's okay?"

Ten minutes later my capris and t-shirt bagged and tagged, an overlarge *Zip It!* sweatshirt hanging almost to my knees over a pair of pajama bottoms from the trunk of my car, I huddled in the entrance building while Dr. Aberstock gave me a quick once over.

"You're fine," he said with that characteristic cheeriness that usually made me feel comforted and instead, today, made me want to smack him. "A bit of rest and you'll be right as rain."

"Thanks," I said through gritted teeth. "Because I'll be sleeping anytime soon." Every time I closed my eyes, I saw Lewis staring back at me. Hello, impending insomnia. Nice to see you.

"Let me know if you need sleeping pills," he said, patting my hand. "In the meantime, if you'll excuse me, I have a body to examine further." He winked at me. "You know how to find the fresh ones, Fee. He's only been gone maybe a half-hour."

Which meant he'd likely died minutes before I'd found him. Awesome. I let the jovial doctor go without questions despite his willingness to share information, not typical of me and my usual nosiness. Except, of course, there was little doubt in my mind what killed Lewis Brown. The rope wrapped tightly around his neck, his bulging eyes and dark red face pretty much told the tale of strangulation before he'd been cut loose to lie in wait for poor, unsuspecting me.

Wait, hadn't Aiden reported some rope missing from the entrance? Sure, Fee, start asking questions. Way to distract yourself. "At least they didn't find any woodpeckers," I said to no one in particular.

Carmen shot me a glare that told me she wished they had instead of a body. That made two of us.

Toby hurried inside, her sweet face pinched and worried, and she took a moment to cup my face in both hands before she settled into the office chair at the back of the building and began reviewing the security tape, Crew hanging over her shoulder. I needed to go home and now that Dr. Aberstock had my clothes and had checked me out I could go. Except, of course, I didn't trust myself to drive just yet.

Not to mention my sense of nosey wasn't going anywhere.

The front door burst open, Grace Perkins barging inside. Robert seemed to have his hands full with her, not to mention the taller, if less aggressive, Philip Davis. The young man who'd run into me earlier caught my eyes for only an instant before his gaze twitched away. Hang on, he'd been hot-footing it from the same direction as the tree where Lewis was found. Was that guilt on his face? He seemed intent on keeping Grace between himself and Carmen who glared at him a moment before looking away.

Grace, meanwhile, sobbed openly, both hands coming down with a loud bang on the front counter. "I demand you arrest these, these," she inhaled a shaking breath, finger-pointing at Carmen and Aiden, "murderers at once!"

Crew's scowl as he turned wasn't aimed at the weeping woman but at Robert whose sullen return frown wasn't doing him any favors. When the sheriff spoke, it was firmly but with compassion.

"Ms. Perkins," he said, "please allow Deputy Carlisle to escort you out. I'll have questions for you shortly."

She shrugged off Robert's hand on her shoulder, Philip edging himself sideways and blocking my cousin's next attempt. While normally Robert's discomfort—especially in the presence of his boss—would make me grin in evil triumph, I could barely muster the ability to give a crap.

"Excuse me," Carmen snapped at Grace who spun on her with a flare of anger behind her tears. Only Philip's hand on her arm kept her from lunging at the young owner of *Zip It!* while the girl spoke. "Did you find any evidence of wrongdoing on our part?" She sounded furious, vibrating with it, her own tears imminent, I was sure. "Any sign of your precious woodpeckers or proof any of us did anything to hurt anyone?" She didn't wait for an answer, her hands falling to fists at her sides, chest heaving as she visibly fought for control of herself. "We have been nothing but accommodating to a pack of rabid trolls, led by you and Mr. Brown, Miss Perkins. And you blame us for his death?" She spun until her back was to the accusing older woman, hands now clenched in front of her. To keep her from striking out? Maybe. I had a temper, so my stomach twisted in empathy for Carmen's battle over her fury. "You've ruined us and for what? For nothing. The same nothing Mr. Brown died for. You have yourself to blame for that."

Grace seemed floored by Carmen's attack, her sobs silenced a moment before she started up again, both hands over her face, wailing loss escaping her fingers as if she tried to contain the sound with that gesture. Philip's arm slipped around her shoulders, his face tight while Carmen took two strides past Robert and exited the room, slamming the door behind her.

"I can't believe he's gone." Grace turned, hugged Philip who embraced her back. "What are we going to do without him?"

The better question was, why did the protestor die the way he did, and for what motive was he killed? While possibly the reason for his untimely end, if Lewis wasn't killed over the woodpecker issue, why was he? Who had it out for him and did it have anything to do with the park? I wrinkled my nose at myself, rubbed my arms with both hands, felt a grin try to pull at my lips despite the situation. I was obviously feeling better.

I followed Carmen outside, needing fresh air and maybe a stiff drink and some way to erase Lewis's staring eyes from my mind, shivering as I exited into the falling afternoon. While it had been a gloriously warm day, it was still May, and the disappearing sun left a chill in the air I wasn't prepared for. I caught sight of Carmen disappearing into the trees and followed her, though I should have gone home. The impulse to try to comfort her came as a surprise, but instead of sourced from my usual busybodiness, it came from a sense of solidarity.

I'd been through what she was going through, had a dead body in my koi pond two weeks after taking over Petunia's. Things might look grim, but I wanted my fellow female entrepreneur to know it wasn't necessarily the end of the world. She deserved a bit of support after all this.

That intent in mind, my knees still a bit weak but

my heart in the right place, I followed Carmen's path, waving to Jill who just shrugged and let me go. It wasn't until I passed beneath the first big maple, the last sunlight flashing over the edge of the mountain rim, I caught the flare of light on glass deeper in the woods. I stopped in my tracks, recognizing the photographer from earlier as Fleur King disappeared in the opposite direction Carmen had.

I didn't think, my best attribute, and immediately shifted course, going after her.

CHAPTER THIRTEEN

I wasn't expecting a companion in my pursuit and almost leaped out of my new sweatshirt when a big hand caught my arm and turned me around before I could make it two strides. I meeped in fear, catching myself from screaming all over again when I realized it was Matt staring down at me, his handsome face tight with concern.

"Fee, where are you going?" His hand slid down to grasp my fingers, holding me in place with that simple touch. "You need to go home, lie down." His free hand touched my cheek, tucked a piece of hair behind my ear. "Do you need a ride? I'm sure the sheriff can spare me if you want me to drive you to Petunia's."

I brushed off the odd feeling in my chest at the attention, shaking my head to clear it. What the hell was wrong with me? Yes, he was cute, and I was a bit of a mess, but seriously. Hormones? At a time like this? "There's a photographer," I blurted. Pointed at the trees. "She's been taking pictures of license plates." That was better, more focused. "She's been lurking around." Not that lurking was illegal and, in all honestly, there had been tons of media in the park today. But Fleur's telephoto lens and previous activity made her suspicious to me.

Matt looked up, followed my pointing with his eye line, then nodded. "I'll take care of it," he said, sounding oddly like some kind of silver screen hero riding into battle. I let him go, eye-rolling to myself, though sagging as I realized he was probably the better choice to pursue her considering the weakness I was feeling all of a sudden.

Stupid adrenaline had to wear off now, didn't it?

But, instead of turning back as he'd likely intended, I instead veered and headed in my original direction, looking for Carmen. I could at least finish what I'd started and do some good before going home to collapse and hug my pug.

The path ahead split, the one on the right going deeper into the park while the left one led to the last tree and the crime scene. I suppressed a shudder but took the left fork, figuring that was likely where Carmen had gone. At least, it would have been my choice if I was her. And the need to poke around as usual outweighed the simmering fear still clinging to me. Maybe if I could find some answers—while comforting the young woman, naturally—I could help myself at the same time.

Sure, Fee. Way to make excuses for sticking your nose into Crew's crime scene.

Though I argued as I forced myself forward, off the side of the path to skirt the tape and under it, it was kind of my crime scene too, right? I stumbled as I circled the big tree that marked the beginning of the last line, my foot catching on something tucked between two roots, and scowled with a surge of disgust at the protest sign leaning haphazardly into the depression formed by the side of the towering tree. A large partial footprint, deep in the damp soil of the root system, seemed oddly out of place. The climbing ladder to the zip line was on the other side of this tree. I looked around, frowning. No one would have any reason to be on the forward side unless.

Unless.

I reached for my phone, realized I'd left it in the car, grumbled to myself a moment while I backed carefully away from the shoe print and the sign. Likely neither had anything to do with the murder but I wasn't taking chances, not now that Crew and I were finally making headway.

"Fee!" Matt came to a panting halt at my side, hand settling on my shoulder. I looked up at him, then pointed at the possible evidence.

"Can you photograph that?" Likely Robert or Jill already had, but still. "Just in case."

Matt whipped out his phone and did the job, speaking in a rather excitable tone as he did. "I lost her," he said, snapping a couple of pictures before tucking his phone away again. I guess he wasn't used to this kind of thing like I was. And that in itself had the kind of hilarity to it that made me want to curl up on the couch with a pint of double chocolate chunk ice cream and drown my sorrows in sugar. He was the one with the gun and the training, after all. "You think she's the murderer?" He sounded so eager, so young.

I shrugged, wondering why I felt like a jaded old PI from a bad movie all of a sudden. "Doubt it," I said, my voice raspy and aching, a perfect fit for the previous mental image. "But she might have some pictures that could help the investigation."

"Right." He practically bounced on his toes as he looked around. "I'll keep looking for her. But we need to get you home." There was that kindness again, that soft, sweet worry. I honestly didn't know what to do about it and instead of trying to figure it out in my present state of mind, I shrugged and let him lead me to the entrance again.

Crew looked up from where he talked with Jill, a faint frown at the sight of me emerging from the trees making me want to sigh in frustration. Wait, Jill seemed to be unhappy about seeing me with Matt, too. What was wrong with people today? I stopped in front of the sheriff, crossing my arms over my chest, wishing I could find that happy sense of light excitement that had dominated the last few hours, feeling cold and tired and dirty instead and just wanting a long shower and Petunia.

"I'm going home," I said. Crew didn't argue, though the glance he shot at Matt told me what he was about to suggest. "I'm fine to drive. I promise." I hesitated while the handsome sheriff leaned toward me, lips almost touching my ear.

"I'll check on you later," he said, deep voice gruff. "Forget about dinner for now." Crap, right, dinner. Damn it, that made my eyes prickle with the need to cry for the lost opportunity, a surefire sign I was in no shape to carry on any kind of mealtime conversation anyway. "Are you sure you're okay?"

I refused to break down. Refused outright and utterly. No freaking way, not right here in front of Jill who seemed nervous and a bit edgy for some reason, and now Robert, Matt and least of all Crew. Nope, not doing it. Instead, I stepped firmly past him and strode like I meant it—like I had the strength to make it to my car without stumbling or collapsing or breaking into sobs—all the way to the blacktop and, miracles never cease, into the driver's seat of my car.

I don't remember starting the engine or pulling out of the parking lot or even finally jerking the wheel over and stopping on the side of the road. I do remember sobbing into my hands for a solid minute out of sight of the park. Though by the time I hunted down an old fast-food napkin to blow my nose and had myself back on the road for home, it was dark enough I had a headache from squinting into the twilight.

Sure, that's where the headache came from.

By the time I pulled in the driveway at Petunia's,

my hands had stopped shaking and I no longer had a deep hitch in my breathing. The last of the hiccups had gone away, too, and I even felt rather optimistic I might be able to pass out and maybe not have a nightmare dominated by bulging dead guy eyes for tonight at least.

I circled to the kitchen door, wanting to avoid my guests if possible and not even really in the mood to talk to Daisy, though I'd have to, eventually. My hope I could sneak inside and downstairs to my apartment, shower—with likely more sobbing and a bit of shaking thrown in for good measure—before pretending I was 100% so I could go back upstairs, didn't turn out the way I planned.

Instead of a quick dodge through to quiet and solitude, I found myself face-to-face with the last person I expected, her eyes that matched mine so wide and worried I instantly lost my final shred of self-control and fell into my mother's arms.

CHAPTER FOURTEEN

Honestly, I was half expecting her to reject me, considering the mood she'd been in lately. But I couldn't help myself and, when Mom's arms clutched me close, her familiar voice whispering in my ear soothing sounds mothers make when their children need comfort, it almost made things worse. I took a long few minutes to just hug her and cry and reconnect to the mom I loved so much while she not only allowed it, she encouraged me.

When I finally pulled away, snuffling and wiping at my nose, I realized we weren't alone, that Daisy stood off to one side, holding a box of tissues in one hand she quickly rushed to offer me when Mom released her tight hold. I helped myself to several, blowing my nose and emptying the last of my stress into the soft sheets before hugging Mom again, kissing her cheek.

"Mom," I whispered in her ear, "I'm so sorry about everything."

"Fee," she whispered back, "so am I." She leaned away, blinking through her own wet lashes before turning to smile at Daisy with the barest amount of brittleness to her expression. Less faking her good humor and more an attempt to pretend she had it together, I think. For my benefit or not, it was just nice to have her there, to feel her hand slide down my arm and find my fingers while she tugged me against her hip. "I'm going to take Fiona downstairs and get her cleaned up." She turned and shook her head at me, though without judgment, tsking softly. "Poor darling, we heard all about it. Are you okay?"

"I am now." I let her lead me through the kitchen, meeting Daisy's wide eyes on the way by, her subtle shrug of confusion at Mom's change of heart, but the delight and mixed worry/anxiety/questioning that I knew would lead to the two of us huddled back up here in short order over coffee while I spilled everything. For now, I followed Mom down to my apartment, only noticing as I did the chubby, fawn creature who bumped into me several times, her head turned upward, black, triangle-shaped ears perked while she whined softly for my attention. I bent and scooped Petunia into my arms, her loss of several pounds the previous winter creeping back toward the portly despite my sign and thanks to the plethora of guests who gave in to her adorably pleading gaze about as far from my mind as could be, just grateful to hug my sweet pug as she gently licked my face.

Mom sat me down at the kitchen island, helping herself to a glass from the cupboard, pouring me a cold glass of water before coming to sit next to me. Her fingers stroked hair back from my cheeks, reminding me oddly of Matt with that gesture, though she distracted me from the memory when she spoke.

"Fee, I'm so sorry this happened to you again," she said. "Did you want to talk about it?"

I shook my head, sipped the water, Petunia trying to lick the side of the glass from her perch in my lap. Unwilling to let her down just yet, I let her balance on my legs while I tried not to spill water all over her. "I really don't," I said with a heavy exhale, Lewis's bugging eyes sharply in mental focus a moment. I coughed on a badly swallowed drop of liquid and took a second to clear my throat before setting the glass down and meeting Mom's eyes. "I'd rather talk about you."

She wrinkled her nose at me, patting my hand, seemed to retreat a moment before returning to nod at me with a faint, embarrassed smile. "I've been... difficult," she said. Laughed a bit too brightly, cheeks pinking. "Oh, Fee. I've been so foolish."

"Mom," I said, "you were purposely betrayed and then publically humiliated for something that wasn't your fault." Defensive of my mother? You betcha. "You earned the time you needed to sort it out."

But Mom wasn't having that. "No," she said, frown forming between her green eyes. "No, Fee, I acted very badly, both to you and your father and I feel terribly about it." She bit her lower lip, hand trembling where it sat on mine. Wow, this was the same woman who lost her crap on me just yesterday. What happened? "There's no excuse for the way I handled that particular disaster. And I wanted to apologize."

I was dying to ask her what changed, but from the way she wavered on the edge of her own breakdown, I decided to leave that particular conversation for another day. I was just happy to have my mother back, thanks. "Accepted," I said, "for what that's worth."

Mom beamed then, flashing a big smile. "I know you've found alternatives, considering how close the wedding is." She shifted on the stool, pulling her hand back, folding both in her lap, though her index fingers twitched like she contained some emotion she couldn't quite hide completely. "But if you need any help at all, I'm happy to contribute. Just say the word."

Okay, so much for not asking. "Mom, of course, I'd love that." Would I. While I was positive we had things well in hand, having my mother to oversee the food would take a massive weight off my shoulders, a weight I didn't realize I carried until I felt it lift and leave me. Not to mention I could finally broach the partner subject I'd been aching to have with her and Daisy. Another huge smile from her lit her up like a sun from within while I smiled back in wonder. "What changed your mind?"

Mom hesitated long enough I knew she didn't want to talk about it. "I had a visitor this morning," she said. And stopped. "Doesn't matter who." Another pause, a deep breath. "Needless to say, that conversation helped me see how silly I've been." Her faint laugh shook. "I've been torturing myself for nothing. And it has nothing to do with the show or the wedding or anything else. It's been all about me, Fee, and my doubts about what I want to do next."

Whoever it was talked Mom from the ledge? I owed them big time. Made me sad, though, knowing I hadn't been able to help her, that it took someone else to do so. Funny how the lives of those I loved actually unfolded around me without my knowledge, assistance or consent. Imagine that—they had their own existence that had nothing to do with me. Snort.

"Mom, I'm sorry, but the cake..." Surely, she knew it had already been ordered this close to the date?

Mom shrugged, smiled like it didn't matter, authentic enough I believed it didn't. "I just want to help, honey," she said.

"Have you talked to Dad?" That would be the icing on my very own dessert, thank you very much. But from the way she flinched, how her smile faded, and she refused to meet my eyes for a long moment I knew she hadn't yet.

"He's busy working," she said, lower lip trembling just enough I knew that conversation would be harder for Mom to broach than this one had been. "Fee, we've said such horrible things to each other." The faint wail behind her words caught up short as she stopped, lips clamping together. "Things I've said." That came out in a whisper. "He'll never forgive me."

Petunia protested as I set her down and hugged Mom, the two of us awkwardly hanging off the sides of the stools where we perched, clinging to each other while I squeezed her tight.

"Dad loves you," I said, knowing my thick voice gave away my emotions as much as my embrace's desperate edge. "He just wants you to be happy."

I waited a heartbeat or two, gave her time to answer, but when she didn't, I drew a breath to prod her. Too late, apparently. Mom let me go and stood, brushing at the front of her jeans with both hands before nodding toward my bedroom.

"We can talk about all of this later," she said. "I'm being selfish, and you've been through so much today, sweetie." She pulled me to my feet. "You need a hot shower and some dinner," she said, brusquely Mom again, the mother I adored taking over, her familiar tone pushing me to my feet and moving me with just her words. "I'll make you something myself."

While I could have argued and tried to convince her I was fine, I wasn't. As selfish as it was, I needed my mom. So, I caved and headed for the bathroom, my aching heart sighing in relief I had my mother back.

CHAPTER FIFTEEN

By the time I showered, pulled a brush through the snarly unhappiness of my thick, auburn hair and dressed in a few layers of fluffy fleece while my shocky body struggled to get warm, Mom had whipped up a lovely dinner of fresh pasta and garlic bread, while Daisy quietly guided the new staff out of the kitchen so Mom and I could be alone. I found I missed the grumpy old ladies who used to work for me, both Betty and Mary Jones retired officially four weeks ago, though they'd agreed to come back from time to time if I needed their help. Things had changed so much, the new cook, Clara, and the four young chambermaids whose names I was still trying to recall (like pinning tails on a donkey sometimes and more often than not got wrong or mixed up) firmly placed on Daisy's list of things to handle so

Fee didn't lose her mind.

I really didn't know what I'd do without her. It seemed like the business stuff—the renovations, managing social media, bookings and keeping Petunia's and the annex supplied—took up so much time I barely had a minute to talk to guests or get to know the staff. I did know I wasn't 100% happy with Clara's cooking, though I didn't want to second guess Daisy and with business booming, I was kind of low on options. That was until Mom handed me this golden opportunity I couldn't pass up.

"How is the new staff working out?" She had that perfect mix of curiosity and longing in her tone that told me I had an opening to further relief beyond assistance with the wedding.

"Mom," I said, knowing I sounded desperate and hoping I didn't push the tone over the edge too far, "I need your help."

The expression on her face told me I'd said exactly the right thing. "Sweetie, anything," she said.

"Clara can handle Petunia's." At least, I hoped so. Daisy rejoined us, sitting next to me and nodding with a smile, but hers was strained.

"It's the annex," Daisy said, shaking out her dark blonde hair, gray eyes worried. "I haven't been able to find anyone to run the kitchen." She pursed her full lips, a faintly guilty look on her face. "I've tried, Fee, but the area is tapped out."

I patted her hand. "You've done amazingly," I said. "I'd never have made this work without you." Her return smile was stronger, but she immediately spun on Mom as if worried the chance at nabbing my mother would disappear in a flash.

"Lucy, you have to take over," Daisy gushed. "You're the only one who can do it."

Mom seemed utterly shocked by that revelation and while I knew we'd be okay if she turned us down—we'd manage somehow, we always did, despite my worries about wearing out eventually— seeing her light up in delight and then settle into Mom to the rescue mode was about as perfect an outcome as I could have asked for.

"You just say the word, girls," she said, ladling some food out for Daisy, too. "I'm yours."

Daisy beamed at her, grasping Mom's hand in hers. "You're a lifesaver."

She wasn't the only one. And sitting there, with the two women I loved most in the world open to possibility, I finally had the chance to broach the idea that had been lurking in my mind and heart for months.

"I can't do this alone," I said, throwing that at them without a trace of self-recrimination, not meaning to sound whiny and hoping I didn't. Mom and Daisy both looked startled, but when my bestie tried to reassure me, I silenced her with a quick, tired smile. "Just listen, okay?" She nodded, Mom pausing to pay attention, while I sat back from my dinner and sighed. "I leaped into this annex thing, thinking I could do it all. But Day, without you, seriously." I exhaled heavily, tension making my shoulders ache. "This whole place would have fallen apart before now." I turned to Mom. "I realized not so long ago I don't need employees. I need partners." Wide eyes met mine. "And I want the two of you to be those partners." Mom gaped at me while Daisy gasped.

"Fee, Petunia's is yours." I'd never seen my best friend so utterly flabbergasted. Expected this reaction, anticipated it. "You don't need me." There was that flash of doubt in her I'd been seeing the last few months, that I knew was going to be my main battle with her. It started when she tried to convince me she wasn't smart enough to figure out Grandmother Iris's puzzle and hadn't gotten better. While I had as yet to source the real cause, it didn't matter, not at this moment. "Not that way. I'm happy to help. But partners?"

"Yes," I said, as firmly as I could, wishing she could see herself the way I saw her. "Here's how I'm imagining it." I pushed a saltshaker into the middle of the counter, pepper beside it, sugar bowl following as I spoke. "There are three arms to this project now. The bed and breakfast," that was sugar, "the bulk of the work and stress for Petunia's to this point. Only made all the more complicated with the rooms at the annex." I tapped the top of the bowl with my fork, making it ring softly. "But now there's events." Salt joined the fat-bottomed container while I thought about all the calls we'd been getting lately about parties and more weddings and a seemingly endless march of requests for special occasion celebrations I hated to turn down. "And third, is catering." Hello, pepper shaker. The three china pieces snuggled together between us, Mom and Daisy staring at them like they had no idea what they were. "Between the three of us, I think we've got it covered." I looked up then, met their eyes while they exchanged looks before turning their attention back to me. "You're crazy to say yes," I laughed then. "I bit off a giant bite of holy crap with this renovation. And I'm absolutely aware of that fact." The thought of dealing with everything alone made me want to throw up. Never mind dead bodies, the stress of the last five months? I was kidding myself if I thought sleepless nights came from death and not impending fear of disaster and failure. "But if you're willing to partner with me, I know we can make it work."

Mom inhaled, paused. "Fee," she said, voice warbling slightly, "I don't want to steal your thunder."

I laughed at that, sagged against the counter in front of me. "Mom," I said, "I've been dying to ask you, even when it was just Petunia's. I didn't originally because I knew you were perfectly capable of finding your own awesome to do. Then the stupid show happened, and…" I left that hanging, turned to Daisy. "As for you, same thing." I hadn't wanted to saddle her with Petunia's despite how awesome she'd been from day one. But she seemed to have chosen to stay. Who was I to argue when I needed her to? "I'm not above begging."

Daisy's hesitation continued. "I can't afford to buy in, Fee," she said, flushing. "You've put so much money into this renovation, I wouldn't want to take advantage of that."

Mom's nod echoed my bestie's sentiment. "I can pull from my pension for both of us," she said, patting Daisy's hand.

Right. They had no idea I'd already thought this through. "I'm not asking either of you to cough up anything," I said. "I'll retain ownership in the original Petunia's and will keep the equity I invested in the annex. But we can share equally in the ownership and debt of the annex moving forward. I'll take a larger share until that debt owed me is paid off." I'd already had a brief chat with my accountant and lawyer about this very thing. All I needed was for these two to agree.

Daisy laughed herself, shaking her head in a dazed way that solidified into a smile so lovely I knew I'd finally helped her shed some of her doubt. She rose and came to my side, hugged me, pulled Mom into the embrace. "We're going to own this town," she said without a hint of malice. Mom's giggle, on the other hand? Adorably wicked and set me off, too.

A few tears and more hugs later and I let them go, the three of us grinning at each other like we'd just made a deal with the devil and got away with it. Well, maybe we had. Time would tell.

"Now," Mom said, filling my plate one more time while Petunia licked her chops and waited for scraps to fall from the spoon, "Fiona Fleming, tell your mother about what happened today. And leave nothing out."

CHAPTER SIXTEEN

It didn't take me long to tell them what I knew, including the fact the two instigators of the protest had been staying right here at Petunia's. I didn't have time to worry about who'd been taking on Lewis's things, not when Daisy immediately rose to offer a call to the sheriff's office to let Crew know the dead man's property was in our possession.

Right, I should have thought of that. Instead of letting her do the deed, I made her sit, leaving her chatting with Mom, and exited to the main foyer to make the call. Surely Crew knew by now that Lewis had been staying here, but I didn't want him to think I was keeping anything from him.

As I lifted the phone to dial, the murmured sound of guests in the dining and sitting rooms filling the background of Petunia's with the now-familiar hum of occupation, the front door opened and the tall, slender photographer I'd been hunting earlier entered. When Fleur King met my eyes, hers widened and she seemed to freeze as if I'd caught her in some act, she wished I hadn't witnessed. Then, an instant later, she relaxed and began to chuckle, crossing to the sidebar where guests checked in.

"Right, this is your place." She looked like she was mentally kicking herself for dropping the ball. Hang on, how did she know anything about me? "Silly of me to forget such a simple thing, but I've been a bit distracted." She grinned then, shrugged. "Apparently I'm not meant to escape you, Detective Fleming," she said with a wink.

That was an odd way to address me. "Miss King," I said. "Take any interesting photos today?"

She grimaced, though her eyes sparkled with good humor. "Wouldn't you like to know?" Her thin face showed only wry amusement so if she'd found something she wasn't going to let me know about it. At least, not yet. "Any room at the inn for a weary traveler?"

"As it turns out," I said, "I had a cancellation." Last-minute back-outs were the bane of my existence, but in this case, I'd forgive the Petersons for forgetting it was their oldest daughter's college graduation this weekend. But would their daughter? "How would you like to pay?"

I took careful note of her ID and credit card. She was, at least, who she said she was. Or her identification confirmed it, though for all I knew both could be fake. When I handed them back, she didn't comment at my careful perusal, still with that sarcastically sly smile on her face.

"Let me escort you upstairs to your suite." It wasn't lost on me I wasn't exactly dressed professionally in my fleece and damp hair, but I wasn't letting her out of my sight just yet. I held out a hand to help her with her bag and she handed me the strap of the long, narrow case I could only guess held her camera without hesitation while she swung a duffle over one shoulder. Was that a challenge in her eyes? I found myself grinning back as I led her upstairs to room six and opened the door for her. The lovely pale red room with its checkerboard gingham pattern always made me think of summer as a girl, though Fleur didn't comment on the décor. Instead, she took her camera bag from me and tossed it to the quilt before dropping her duffle on the carpet.

"You have questions," she said, though why she'd know or care was beyond me. "So do I."

Interesting. "You missed evening dinner service," I said, "but if you're hungry, feel free to join me in the kitchen. End of the foyer, just come straight through."

She nodded, hands sliding into the hip pockets of her jeans while she observed me like she expected something different and wasn't sure what to think. "I'll be right down."

Okay then. I retreated, a bit confused by her attitude. I barely had time to warn Mom and Daisy she was on her way when Fleur appeared at the swinging door, an easy smile on her face though her eyes remained guarded while she shook hands, messenger bag slung across her narrow chest. Was it just me or did she seem far too familiar with us, even bending to pat Petunia? Not that the pug was complaining.

Mom served Fleur before hooking her arm through Daisy's, eyes meeting mine. "Let's slip across to the annex," she said to my best friend. "I have some things I want to chat about before the wedding." It was pretty obvious she was leaving so I could question Fleur and I let her, Daisy arching her eyebrows at me as the pair disappeared out the kitchen door, the sound of their voices fading while Petunia ignored their departure in favor of the possibility of shared snacks.

I fed her sliced strawberries from the fridge while Fleur ate a few bites.

"Delicious," she said, sounding surprised. "I'd heard your mother was a great cook."

Heard from whom? "She's the best." I meant that.

"Nice to see she's recovered from the debacle in January." Fleur seemed amused by my confusion, which only triggered my temper.

"You seem to know a lot about my mother," I said, knowing it came out snappy.

Fleur shrugged, utterly unaffected by my show of irritation. "Not just your mother," she said. "Your reputation precedes you, Fiona Fleming."

Grunt. "What does that mean?"

Fleur chewed and swallowed, offering Petunia a tiny morsel of chicken before resting her elbows on the counter and sighing. "I make a point of researching everyone I'm going to encounter while I'm working a story," she said. "And I have to admit, I'm equally horrified and impressed by what I've found out about your little town."

Story? "You're a writer?"

"Photojournalist," she said. "I've been digging into the mysterious Reading, Vermont for months now, and the equally curious Fiona Fleming." Her eyes sparkled. "Tell me, Fee, just why it is you seem to be in the middle of so many murders?"

Wait, she was here for me? "I had nothing to do with any of them." Defensive, really? I had nothing to hide.

Fleur laughed, went back to her dinner. "I didn't say you did." She grinned at me. "But you have to admit it's a gigantic coincidence, isn't it? And I don't really believe in coincidence. Which makes me ask the question, what is it about you, in particular, that attracts murder?"

She wasn't exactly endearing herself at the moment. "Tell you what," I said, "when I find the answer to that question, I'll give you a call." Snarl.

Fleur raised one hand, shook her head, sardonic smile fading. "I'm just observing," she said. "No harm meant, honestly. But you do have to admit, it's rather odd. The increase in the death toll in Reading? A town where the last murder happened before you were born?" She hesitated, eyes narrowing. "Investigated by your father, I believe. And never solved to anyone's satisfaction."

I didn't know that. "If you're here to investigate me, you're going to need a lawyer."

She finished her plate of pasta, slurping up the last noodle, wiping at the sauce with the heel of bread Mom had supplied. "I'm not," she said. "I mostly investigate environmental issues these days. It was just brought to my attention I might get the opportunity to ask you some questions."

"I'm not interested." Wow, grumpy thy name is Fiona Fleming.

Fleur watched me a long moment, wiping her mouth with her napkin, before reaching into her bag and pulling out a tablet. She gestured for me to join her and, naturally, my nosiness wasn't going to let me stand idly by without finding out what she was up to. A moment later, she showed me a handful of correspondence from a number of journalists whose names I didn't know but all of whom mentioned me.

"Just chatter," she said then. "Mostly because of a mutual friend, I believe."

My heart stuttered to a stop, sense of betrayal hitting like a blow at the sight of Pamela Shard's name.

Fleur didn't seem to notice my anxious reaction. "I knew Pam in Boston when she worked *The Globe* as an investigative journalist. Back when she was a big deal." Fleur seemed disappointed.

Wait, Pamela was what? "How long ago was

that?" I knew some of Pamela's background, mostly because of the death of Sadie Hatch and her history with the fake psychic. And, of course, her broken heart over Aundrea's forced marriage to Pete. But I had no idea she'd had any kind of big career behind her.

"A shame, really," Fleur sighed, ignoring my question to answer as she liked. "She was a powerhouse not so long ago. Shocked everyone when she just up and left Boston like she did." Including Fleur? Maybe more than shock if the woman's edge of hurt was any indication. She covered it well, but not completely.

"Love makes you do things no one expects," I said while Fleur grinned suddenly, painfully.

"Yeah, I heard about that. Well, I don't begrudge her a happily ever after." The young photographer seemed like she wanted to say more, that lingering bit of sadness behind her eyes, but she shrugged it off. "Anyway, because of Pam's past, a lot of people I know read the *Reading Reader Gazette*." She apparently found that funny because a snort escaped. "Is your mayor really that much of a hardass about parking?"

She had no idea. The next time Robert gave me a gleeful ticket for parking on the street outside my own B&B (five minutes to run things inside was not parking, thank you very much) I was taking my grievance to Olivia's office personally. At least my feelings of betrayal were fading. So, Pamela wasn't talking about me per se. That was a relief. I wasn't sure how I'd face her if she'd been playing me false.

"Just so you know," Fleur said, "Pam seems to think you're the go-to when it comes to crimes in Reading," she said, tucking her tablet away again. "That the local sheriff is a bit of a plodding perfectionist, and his deputies can't find a clue if it lands in their laps." I wanted to protest, to defend Crew, but I was still stunned by the fact Pamela was talking about me. "Though, from what I understand, your father—former Sheriff Fleming, right?—has his own network now that he's become a P.I. So, I'll be paying him a visit, too. But I hadn't planned on talking with either of you before I had something concrete to work with."

"What does that mean?" I sank to a stool and waited for her to go on, knowing I had to be pale and feeling my pulse slowly return to normal. I'd be having a firm talk with Pamela over this.

"Only that I hadn't meant to encounter you the way I did." Fleur sounded almost apologetic. "Sorry to be so cloak and dagger, but it's a small place and I didn't want to show my hand too soon."

"You're here because of what, the woodpeckers?" Now that I wasn't so freaked out about Pamela I found I was a bit too curious about Fleur's secretive lifestyle. A photojournalist? Actually, kind of awesome.

"No," she said, face grim now, hands clasped on the counter in front of her. "I've been tracking Lewis Brown."

His bulging, dead eyes flashed in my head. Eep. Fleur seemed to realize mentioning him brought me discomfort because she watched me with a cool, level gaze while I swallowed past the need to squirm.

"Why?" Did Fleur have an idea who might have killed him?

But rather than spill everything, she winked. "That's my scoop," she said, sitting back, grinning. "The story I came for. And his death just adds layers to the truth." She hesitated before her face cleared of the secret, closed expression she'd been wearing since I'd met her, a flash of youthful enthusiasm showing through. "Don't suppose you'd let me have a peek through his things before the cops come for them, would you?" She laughed. "One girl to another?"

Yeah, like that was going to happen. "Don't suppose you want to tell me why you're investigating him?" I winked right back.

Fleur's face shuttered again but there was no animosity in her. "I'm going to go chat with Pam. But I'm hoping if you come across anything interesting you might be open to a bit of an information swap." She stood swiftly, shouldering her bag before shrugging. "Or not. I'm cool either way. Just keep it in mind if you would."

She departed without another word, leaving me to stare after her like she hadn't just handed me the business end of a venomous snake. Because there was no way I could resist exchanging clues, not even at the risk of Crew's wrath. And Fleur clearly knew that truth.

Pamela was in so much trouble.

CHAPTER SEVENTEEN

Mom and Daisy arrived back in the kitchen shortly after Fleur left, both eager to find out what was going on. After another quick fill-in session, I sat at the counter with a queasy feeling in my stomach while Mom sighed over what I told her.

"Our little town was bound to catch some attention, dear," she said. "After all, with the death of Skip Anderson, we had a rather giant spotlight shone in our direction. Then with Ron's death in January? And considering you've been in the middle of every murder, well." She looked like she wanted to take back what she just said. "I'm sorry, sweetie. It's not your fault."

Daisy hesitated before blurting (because she was clearly taking lessons from me). "Some people are saying it's Olivia's fault." She clasped both hands over her mouth as if she'd said something sacrilegious.

Mom sighed, patted her arm. "I've heard the same thing, Daisy," she said. "People are pointing fingers at her, saying the increase in tourist traffic is to blame for the rise in the crime rate." I hadn't paid attention to such things, but had other crimes been on the rise? "Whatever the case," Mom said then, "there's not much to be done by way of complaining at this point." She nodded once like that should solve everything.

She was right, though. We'd made our particular bed here in town, me included. Though if murder was a natural byproduct of increased tourism, I wasn't sure it was worth it.

Thinking about crime led me to thinking about Irish mob boss Malcolm Murray, our own local criminal element. That led to the business card with Siobhan Doyle's name written on it which just made me flush in guilt with my mother standing in front of me. Prodded the need to make a call to the woman about my father, something Malcolm seemed to think I should have done long ago. I almost told my mother, asked her what it meant, but apparently, she took my upset as something else entirely because she hugged me quickly while Daisy spoke up.

"Are you going to tell Crew?" Darn it, I hadn't even called him about Lewis's room, I'd been so distracted by Fleur's arrival. And yes, I really needed to. Which made me laugh and shrug.

"He's a smart cookie," I said. "I imagine he's

already looking into Lewis Brown's past. Whatever that reporter is digging into, I'm sure Crew will find it, too." Or I'd be passing on what I learned from her.

"He is indeed," Mom said with a reassuring pat to my hand. "And so are you, honey."

My mother. So sweet.

When Mom finally left a short time later, excited chatter about new recipes and the partnership making all that was my mother right in the world again, I turned to find Daisy standing in the kitchen with a book in her hands, a frustrated look on her beautiful face. I knew the book instantly, of course, had read it cover to cover myself several times over the last few months, knew Daisy had, too. The same one we'd gone in search of in January, the one we'd lifted from the Reading Library in search of the treasure my Grandmother Iris sent us after from the grave. Daisy offered it to me with a soft groan and a little grin while I smoothed the plastic-coated film protecting *The Reading Hoard: Fact or Fiction* from harm.

"It's a dead-end," Daisy said, exasperation clear in her voice. "Or the message I found from Iris was a red herring." She seemed about to slip into her "I'm stupid and can't possibly be right" mode all over again.

Yeah, not happening. "We're on the right track," I said. "We just need to know what we're looking for." The book contents were pretty generic, more like it was written for young adults than any serious historian. I'd thought a few times about taking it to Oliver Watters about the author, James Markham, but both Daisy and I hesitated about including anyone else in the mystery. Somehow the joyful delight of January's discovery lingered despite our mutual frustration.

So fun to have this delicious secret between us. And from the sparkle in her gray eyes, Daisy hadn't lost any of her enthusiasm.

"We'll figure it out," she said. "Together." Winked. "Before Mr. Lightmews finds out we stole it."

I laughed over the pinched, older librarian who'd glared at us the entire time we'd giggled and whispered and hushed each other that January afternoon, smuggling the book out of his domain like a pair of juvenile delinquents. The most fun I'd had in a long time, and I wasn't about to give it up now. And while we'd been super busy the last four months, it had been a happy touchstone between us I couldn't bring myself to let go of.

So, what if we never found the treasure? Our private investigation was the point, as far as I was concerned.

I sent Daisy home for the night, trotting downstairs to deposit the book on the kitchen counter in my apartment, lingering over the ship on the cover, the rendering of Captain Reading before drifting back upstairs to finish off some paperwork. Shortly after 10PM, with all of my guests returned and retired, I set up the call bell on the sidebar before going downstairs for the night myself. Daisy's idea, it saved me from wondering if anyone needed me, linked to an app through the computer and to my phone.

I hadn't heard from Crew, kicked myself I failed to call him yet, knew it was too late. He was clearly busy and calling him now felt like I was chasing him instead of trying to be helpful. Instead, I convinced myself to go to the sheriff's office in the morning and see him personally.

Worried I'd struggle with sleep, to my shock, I curled up and passed out about a minute after my head hit the pillow, the softly snoring pug at my side soothing me with the rumbling inhale and exhale of her breathing.

It wasn't until I woke the next morning, the alarm stirring me, I realized I'd been spared nightmares despite the horrors of the day before. Grateful, rested, a shower and a quick bowl of oatmeal chased with coffee later and I returned upstairs with an optimistic feeling despite the murder I'd been so intimately connected to.

It wasn't until my phone rang at 8:30AM, Aundrea's name flashing, I felt my mood deflate. I'd worried she'd turn into Bridezilla and she hadn't failed me, her almost constant calls enough to make me want to hide and let Daisy deal with her. I scooted past Rebecca (or was it Suzie? Crap, maybe her name was Megan) who carried a full tray of Clara's pancakes into the dining room, offering her a weak smile and a brief hello without attempting to use her name and answered the call bound to ruin my morning.

I seriously had no idea. "Fee! Please you have to do something." Aundrea's near panic clenched my stomach into a tight ball of now what. "You have to talk to him, this is ridiculous."

"What's wrong, Aundrea?" I pushed through the kitchen door, dodging (Amber? No, this was Megan, right? Sigh.) as she hurried past with a jug of fresh coffee and a bright smile on a face no older than eighteen. Was I ever that young? "Is this about the flowers?" Wait, no, she'd said "he." He who?

"It's not the wedding," she snapped, her voice near tears. "It's Jared." Um, what? "You need to talk to the sheriff." I almost asked why but she was too fast for me. "Crew's arrested him and he's in jail right now."

This again. I drew a breath, heart racing despite myself. "Aundrea," I said her name slowly, one syllable at a time. "Just take a second. It's going to be okay."

"It's *not*, Fee," Aundrea wailed. "My poor baby didn't do anything."

"You thought Crew arrested Pamela back in October, remember?" All the sheriff wanted to do was ask her questions about her past with Sadie Hatch. "I'm sure everything is fine." While I liked Aundrea, she was a bit of a drama queen.

A bit? Snort.

"You don't understand," Aundrea hiccuped her way through a painful sob. "He's not accusing him of murder." At least there was that. "Jared was in a fight and Crew arrested him and put him in that wretched cell and he's been there all night." She wept a moment while I gaped at my phone. He what? "Please, you have to do something. He'll listen to you."

Thank goodness Daisy came walking through the door, Mom at her side, at that exact moment. I hung up on Aundrea, babbled a quick apology to my mother and bestie before dodging for the door, leaving the hurt and unhappy Petunia behind while I ran the few blocks to the sheriff's office, heart in my throat.

Okay, so it wasn't life or death, but this was Jared and I owed him. If he'd been in lockup all night... not that I'd put some constructive quiet time past Crew if he thought Jared needed it, but town jail?

I took the steps two at a time to the sound of someone shouting within, pretty sure I knew exactly who to expect and threw the door open. I burst into the office to find Aundrea, Pamela holding her back, screaming like a banshee at Crew while Alicia hovered on the periphery, her eyes locked on her boyfriend. He sat on a bunk behind the bars of the small cell on the other side of the divide between reception and the bullpen, head in his hands, looking defeated. In the second cell, separated by a row of bars, Philip Davis sat with his arms crossed over his chest, glaring at the back of Crew's head like he could kill him with his thoughts.

From the black eye and blood on his shirt, it was

pretty clear who Jared had been fighting with.

Crew's eyes lifted from Aundrea and met mine, the faint tic making his cheek jump, vein standing out in his forehead. At least it wasn't me eliciting that response this time, though I was sure my appearance wasn't helping any. Thing was, whether he knew it or not, I was on his side this time.

It took me a moment to get between him and Aundrea, to hug her, to murmur things to her that calmed her down enough she wasn't yelling anymore. Instead, she hugged me back at last and glared at the sheriff while I gently extracted her and handed her off to Pamela. At least the newspaperwoman didn't look pissed, more amused than anything, though Alicia seemed heartbroken enough I reached out and took her hand, tugging her toward me as I addressed Crew in as calm a tone as I could.

"Sheriff Turner," I said.

"Miss Fleming." His jaw jumped.

"I'm wondering if the two you have locked up might not be cooled off enough after a night behind bars to warrant their release." Look at me, the voice of reason. Crew's narrowed eyes softened just slightly. "Good behavior and all that?"

"Still waiting for that good behavior," Crew said while Philip snarled something nasty I didn't quite catch.

"I see." I hugged Alicia before handing her off to her future mother-in-law. "Maybe I could be of some assistance in this instance?" I gestured at Jared who hadn't moved. "If that would be okay with you?"

His lips quirked just a bit, enough I knew he wasn't going to argue. The jumping muscle under his eye eased, the vein relaxing somewhat. "You try a jailbreak and you're going in there with them."

I winked, doing my best to lighten the mood further. "No promises, copper."

Crew's arms dropped from where he'd crossed them over his chest, an immovable force of nature bending. Imagine that. "I won't be pressing charges," he said over my shoulder at Aundrea and Alicia, both of whom seemed mollified. "But I can't have open brawling in the streets, Ms. Wilkins." Aundrea nodded. "Just get them to stop being idiots," he whispered to me on the way by. "If at all possible." He sounded frustrated, annoyed. I paused long enough to grasp his forearm and squeeze gently, hoping he took it as the support I intended.

I just wished I could have done more, especially when the front door banged open again, this time allowing the furiously snarling Olivia Walker entry into his domain. I felt him tense immediately, all of the ground I'd gained with him lost as she stomped to a halt next to Aundrea.

"Sheriff Turner," the mayor snapped, "I'm holding you personally responsible for the disaster at *Zip It!*. You get that park open again or your job is gone!"

CHAPTER EIGHTEEN

Oh, no, she did *not* just threaten him. I might have respected Olivia on professional grounds, but she could back off the guy I was into—especially considering he had the most thankless job in all of Reading, cleaning up the messes she created for him.

Before I could leap to his defense and likely annoy the crap out of him because he was, after all, a big boy who could take care of himself, he did just that, facing off with the mayor with the kind of steady confidence I had learned to adore about him. And make me acutely aware of how mercurial my own temper was in comparison.

Hey, I'd just spent some up close and personal time with a dead guy. Cut me some slack.

"Mayor Walker," he said, deep voice low and level, carrying to everyone in the room, "threatening me is unnecessary. I'm as committed as you are to the safety and protection of this town, despite what you might think to the contrary." That shut her up as a slow flush darkened her paled-out cheeks while she stammered something that might have been an attempt at an apology if he'd given her time to get it all out. "I'm in the middle of investigating the murder at the very park you mentioned, without the kind of backup I could use from state police I might add, at your insistence. And so, I would ask you with great respect to back the hell off so I can do this job you seem to think is at risk."

Wow, color me impressed. Olivia grumbled something I didn't catch but took a step back, nodded.

"You understand my concern," she said.

"I do," he said, hands on hips in an easy posture of control, not a hint of the jaw-grinding annoyance I expected from him in that moment, nor the straining sign of the cords in his neck, the tic under one eye, the vein on his forehead. Good for him for showing such restraint, at least with her. Nice to know I had the ability to get under his skin, I guess.

Olivia swallowed, cleared her throat. "The press—"

"We've had bad press before," Crew said, softer this time, almost kind. Was he empathizing with the pressure she was under or manipulating her? Didn't matter, did the job. She seemed to soften further as he went on. "And we've done okay, as far as I can tell. Let me handle this. You've got enough on your own plate. But until we're done collecting evidence, Olivia, I need to keep the park closed."

Her brown eyes snapped with anger. "No troopers." She shook her head as if calling help would mean some kind of disaster instead of making his life easier. "No outsiders."

He didn't sigh but I could tell from the intake of breath and the sudden tightness of his shoulders he wanted to. "Your call," he said.

Her two companions seemed unhappy with her choice. I only now noticed Olivia hadn't entered alone, so focused on her attack on Crew and the subsequent conversation I only then realized she'd barged in with two town councilors in tow. Sophia met my eyes and seemed irritated to find me there, but Geoffrey Jenkins just nodded and grinned in a way that made me feel like I'd somehow agreed to something I'd regret later.

"Maybe a call to John Fleming is in order," Geoffrey said, turning his attention to Crew.

The sheriff stiffened immediately, though I was pretty sure he didn't intend to show his flash of anger because that steady calm returned, too late. The smirk on Geoffrey's face made me want to smack it off him for that jab at Crew's confidence.

"If I have need for a private investigator," Crew said then, slow and careful, "I'll do just that."

"I for one have all the confidence in the world you'll uncover the truth," Geoffrey said, the pompous ass, two seconds after challenging the sheriff's abilities by throwing my dad at him. He came to stand next to Olivia, one hand falling on her shoulder in a clear show of superiority, if only to me. "The entire council stands behind you and your track record, Sheriff Turner," he said, oily and slick with the kind of subtlety free politicospeak that brought out the worst in me. Olivia blanched then scowled up at him while he finished. "Anything you need." He squeezed Olivia's shoulder, smiled down at her. "Anything."

If it wasn't clear to her before, surely it had to be now, as it was to me and everyone else in the room. Here was the challenging contender in Olivia's next race for mayor. And I was pretty sure he was at least a two step down, thanks.

Crew didn't take the bait, just nodded. "If you'll all excuse me, I have a murder to solve."

Geoffrey didn't give the mayor the chance to argue, using his hand on her shoulder to turn her around and steer her toward the door, Sophia Bell following in annoyed silence. Since she was the only one he'd brought, it was obvious who his main supporter had to be on the council but I wondered how many of the others would be swayed by today's events and the overt signals Geoffrey seemed to be giving off. How long had this undermining of her authority been going on? I really needed to pay attention to local politics.

Crew turned toward me as they left, head down, Aundrea and Pamela, Alicia between them, muttering to each other while the sheriff noticed me standing there. I reached out with one hand, heart in my throat, wanting to support him but not knowing what to say. The sudden breach of his defenses seemed to make things worse for him as he realized I was still there. Whatever anger he'd held inside in the face of opposition from the mayor and her council he seemed suddenly unable to contain. But instead of letting it out at them, he aimed it at me.

"Five minutes, Fee," he snarled, keeping his voice down but enough fury in his tone I knew pushing him would end badly. Why was he taking it out on me? "Then I want you out of here."

My jaw tightened, my own temper waking in reaction. Totally not fair, and despite the fact I knew he wasn't really angry with me it was hard not to feel hurt. But to my credit, rather than taking a bite out of him like I might have not so long ago, I forced a breath into my lungs and clamped down on the need to snap back.

"Ask Matt about the shoe print and sign I found at the base of the tree." I was sure he knew about it already, but I had to bring it up.

Crew's blue eyes snapped fire as he closed the distance between us, lips almost touching my ear. "Fee," he growled, "I will not tell you to mind your own business because I'm done with that." I heard him swallow, felt the heat off his skin as he struggled with his temper. "But I swear to you on this badge I wear if you make trouble for me, I'm going to kick your ass. You hear me?"

I nodded. "Got it."

Crew backed off, nodded himself once, staring at

the floor before turning and striding into his office, not quite slamming the door behind him. I could have gone after him, was tempted. With his searing emotions out of the way compassion washed through me, the understanding he hadn't been exaggerating about the pressure he was under hitting me harder than his temper, wondering just how much weight Dad and I added to his shoulders, especially my father. Instead, I decided to focus on what I could do instead of making Crew's life miserable and spun toward the cells.

Five minutes, huh? Fine. I could accomplish a lot in five minutes. But first, I had three women to wrangle. I could do that much for Crew.

I crossed back to the reception area, the swinging gate hitting my hip as I stopped next to Pamela. Aundrea was near tears, Alicia, too and I hugged them both before forcing a smile.

"It's going to be fine," I lied openly, having no idea if it would or not but needing them to buy it. "I'll talk to Jared. I know Crew will let this go once everyone cools down." More make-believe and guesswork but seemed to do the trick. Then again, I was pretty sure the sheriff would do as he said earlier and not force the issue as long as the two idiots in the cells stopped making his job more complicated.

Aundrea hugged me before casting a longing, sad gaze at her son who sat with his head still in his hands, totally ignoring everything going on past the bars keeping him from freedom. Alicia went with her as they exited, both pausing a few times to look back, then disappeared out the door while I reached out and grabbed Pamela's hand, keeping her with me a moment.

She met my eyes with a faint frown, though she didn't seem worried, more relaxed about the whole debacle that just unwound than she should have been, in my opinion. Instead of calling her on it, I spoke.

"*Boston Globe*, huh?"

She blinked, startled. "That was a while ago," she said.

"Tell that to Fleur King," I said.

Another blink then a grin. "Fleur's in town? Investigating what?"

I shrugged. "Hoping you can find out details and tell me. Something to do with Lewis Brown."

Her eyes narrowed, thin smile dominating her face. "I'll look into it," she said, "and get back to you." Considering all I'd shared with her in the past, I'd be holding her to that. She glanced at Jared with a softening amusement mixed with concern. "Take care of him, yeah? I'm getting kind of fond of the kid."

I nodded, let her go. Watched her leave before turning back to the bullpen and the silent young Wilkens. Crew might have been ready to kick my ass for interfering, but I was in the mood for a boot or two of my own and Jared was in my sights.

CHAPTER NINETEEN

I came to a halt outside the bars, grasping them and staring into the cell. Jared's dark blue t-shirt was torn at the neck, a smudge of dirt on one cheek as he finally looked up and met my eyes. I realized then as I took in the split skin on his right hand over his knuckles and the ashamed expression on his face, I didn't have to give him a hard time over fighting.

He had been doing the job for me all along.

"Hey," I said, keeping it light despite my previous desire to smack him for being an idiot. "How was your night?"

He snorted softly, expression showing faint amusement before he settled back into self-judgment. A quick glance to his left at the scowling Philip told me he wasn't over his anger with his opponent, however.

"I've had worse," he said. Sighed. "And better."

"Mind telling me what the hell you were thinking starting a fistfight with a suspect while a murder investigation is going on?" Might have been a stretch. I had no idea if Crew suspected Philip of anything, though personally, I had him at the top of my own list. I'd seen him hurrying away from the tree where we found—where I'd found—Lewis Black and he'd appeared out of sorts at the time. Never mind Carmen had been right behind him, so was she complicit or guilty even? Of course, I had no proof. Still, stabbing in the dark was a favorite pastime of mine and I wasn't about to stop speculating until I had an answer anytime soon.

Jared's face flinched, flat and angry a moment. "It's personal," he said. "Nothing to do with the murder." Another glare, one that Philip returned before looking away again.

Boys. "Fine, whatever," I snapped. "But you might want to think about putting your private issues to the side while one of your businesses is in trouble. Not to mention hurting your mother and your girlfriend in the process." Okay, not entirely fair, but I wasn't above cheating a little on the emotional manipulation front to get what I wanted.

Jared flinched but didn't relent. "Please stay out of it, Fee."

I tsked at him before spinning on Philip. "You're not talking either, I take it?"

The young protestor flashed me a very rude hand gesture before crossing his arms over his chest again and looking in the other direction.

Perfect. I was done wasting my time on this anyway.

I hesitated as I turned to leave, thinking about Crew. Instead of bothering him directly, I waved to Toby and headed for the street, pausing to text the sheriff instead from the safety of the sidewalk.

I'm so sorry. I had no idea until now what's been going on. I know you told me you were under pressure. I just didn't get it. You weren't kidding. I wish there was something I could do to make it right. I hit send and stood there, chewing my bottom lip, wondering if I should have stayed quiet instead of reaching out, doubting with every passing second before finally hitting regret. Just as my phone chimed and his answer appeared.

You want a job, Fleming?

Um, that was the last response I was expecting. *I'm a bit busy at the moment. Besides, we have this great sheriff in town, and he's got things handled.*

Another pause, shorter this time. *We'll see. About all of it.*

Well, crap. I agonized over sending another text, about turning around and going inside, breaking his no hugging or kissing at the office rule, when a final message landed.

Tell your dad I'll be in touch.

And that was it. I fought the flicker of anger I felt at his text, not sure why it pissed me off as much as it did. Instead of confronting him about it when I had no idea of the context—hey, adulting and not flying off at the handle without all the information necessary, you suck—I tucked my phone into my purse and strode off for Petunia's. Maybe he was really looking for help and maybe he was being a jerk out of a need to let his own temper out but whatever the reason I wasn't in the right state of mind to talk to him about it.

Restraint. I was the picture of restraint. Yup.

To my credit, I also refrained from marching myself to Olivia's office to chew her out over how she'd been treating Crew. Nor did I do the same to Geoffrey Jenkins at his accounting firm downtown. I even held back from kicking the rather large pebble that got in my way as I crossed the street to my B&B despite the fact the stupid thing was clearly asking for it and deserved a good toe launch into next weekend. Instead, I went inside with my need to scream and throw things firmly in check and went back to work.

Walking right into the sight and sound of Grace Perkins arguing with Daisy while Jill winced an apology.

CHAPTER TWENTY

Grace spun toward me while I entered, looking harried and more than a little upset. "They've kicked me out of my room," she snapped like it was my fault. "They're taking Lewis's things!"

Whoops, forgot to mention that to Crew in the kerfuffle this morning. Didn't need to, apparently, though the fact Jill was here now instead of last night made me wince. Hopefully, Crew wouldn't hold my silence against me, or I'd have to stumble through an apology and explanation that likely would just make things worse.

Much more interesting at the moment than my frustrating lack of ability to do the right thing by him was the fact the two activist leaders had been sharing, had they? I didn't realize Grace and the dead guy were a couple. Winced as I accepted she'd not only lost her partner in protest but her boyfriend in the process. Funny, but I struggled with empathy regardless. "I'm sorry to hear that," I said, meeting Daisy's eyes, not even remotely sorry, honestly, after the twenty-four hours I'd had.

"You must find me another room," Grace said like this was my fault. I flashed a scowl at Jill who didn't comment, going upstairs without another word while a pair of guests passed her, concern on their faces.

Great, just what I needed. Meanwhile, Grace launched into a high-volume rant at Daisy while the happy couple I'd checked in earlier scooted out my front door like they dodged a bullet.

Snarl, grumble, argh. "Of course, we can accommodate you," I said, hurrying forward to nod to Daisy, then to Grace with about as fake a smile as I could muster. "Right this way." The last thing I wanted was for the wailing old activist to cause trouble for my guests. And while the house itself was full, I had a couple of days before the wedding, so the annex it was.

"I'll be needing a room for my friend, as well," Grace said then, flipping from whining and annoying to commanding nasty in a heartbeat.

She would, would she? "And who would that be?"

"Philip Davis," she sniffed at me. "Now, my new room? Really, the service in this establishment has been absolutely wretched."

Teeth grinding together, temper rising yet again,

the only thing that kept me from going off? Not the ridiculous belief that the customer was always right. Forget that. I'd booted guests in the past for being rude to Daisy or being generally unpleasant. No, it was the way Fleur emerged from the kitchen, spotted Grace, flinched, then dodged back through the door as if she didn't want the complaining older woman to see her.

That was enough incentive for me to keep Grace around, like it or not. Because whether Fleur intended my curiosity to flare in that moment or not, she succeeded.

I marched Grace across the backyard to the annex back door and led her inside, hating that the first guest in this amazing space would be someone I'd rather camp on the curb with her heavy luggage and a sayonara sucker wave good riddance. Instead, I found myself leading her down the back hall to one of the smaller rooms, refusing to sully the annex further and tucking her in on the first floor beside the kitchen.

The sound of footfalls and voices silenced any protest she might have offered, and I emerged to find Daisy leading Philip into the foyer of my new space. The movers had removed the cardboard protection of my gorgeous floors and his heavy boots left smears of mud on the polished surface. He looked irritated by the whole business, and he wasn't the only one. My poor hardwood. I scowled up at him as I shooed Daisy off, mimicking the crossed arms posture he'd offered me while in his jail cell not so long ago.

"You cause one scrap of trouble in my house, and you'll find your protesting butt bounced onto the street." I gestured at the staircase on impulse, deciding separating Grace from Philip might be a good idea. "Up."

Grace emerged from her room to scowl after me, but I ignored her, opening one of the upstairs rooms for him before stopping to watch him manhandle his bags inside. He didn't seem all that appreciative, the jerk.

"I'll be back with sheets and towels." The rooms weren't even made up yet, damn it. "Don't make a mess. Your stay is temporary." At least, in my house.

Philip turned his back on me without a word and I left him to his silence, hurrying back across the yard to Petunia's for supplies. This was a disaster, I realized, as I dug into the linen closet for what I needed. The annex was supposed to be pristine. If anything happened before the wedding, Aundrea would have a stroke.

Breathe, Fee. What was the worst that could happen? Well, a possible murderer who fist fought with my friend was staying there. How about another dead body? Ooh. If he slept on that new mattress without sheets, I'd murder him myself.

When I emerged from the second-floor closet with an armload of whites, hating the anxiety that buzzed through me over the potential for mess in the annex, I brushed off the young woman who tried to take them from me—hmmm, Chloe? Whatever, I was over it—knowing I wasn't being kind but unable to muster nice right now. In fact, when I trotted downstairs and spotted Jill and Matt in the foyer, seeing them with their uniforms cluttering my entry and the looks on guests' faces who emerged from the dining room to such a view? Yeah, lit me up like nothing else.

But I didn't get to snap at them about tromping their big gun-toting selves into my business like they weren't freaking out my paying customers. Instead, the odd look on Matt's face when he looked up silenced me, made even more uncomfortable by the awkward smile on Jill's while she stared at him.

Oh, dear. So, Jill had a thing for Matt? I'd seen glimmers of it earlier, the clumsy way she'd been around him at the park, how she'd seemed irritated by his attention to me. But damn if it wasn't apparent as hell now. Except that Matt wasn't paying a moment's notice to her, was he? His big eyes stared right at me, the same crooked smile from yesterday that gave me a bit of a guilty thrill tugging at his lips, one big hand holding out a limp hunk of fabric.

"You forgot this at the park," he said. "Just returning it."

Right, the hoodie I'd had tied around my waist. I'd somehow lost it in the kerfuffle, maybe even dropped it when I was zip-lining. I finished my descent and accepted it from him, feeling the tension in the foyer notch upward while silence fell over the three of us, Jill looking at Matt, Matt looking at me and me, well. Me just wanting them both to go away already.

Matt finally cleared his throat. "I guess I should get back." He tipped his hat to me, totally ignoring Jill before nodding and leaving with a sadly hopeful look on his face. How had I missed it? He hadn't even been on my radar since I got home to Reading and all of a sudden, he was into me? Or had he been all along and only now that I was thrown into contact with him I was seeing it?

How much else was I missing by being totally clueless about the people around me?

Jill's soft sigh caught my attention and I spun on her, horrified. "Jill," I said, not knowing what else to blurt out, though a thousand scenarios unfolded in the heartbeat before her sad expression smoothed out and she grinned like it was no big deal.

"Sorry to intrude like this, Fee," she said, one hand settling on the handle of what had to be Lewis Brown's suitcase. "I should get this back to the office. The room's sealed for now until we can finish looking around if that's okay." She left without another word, her blonde ponytail bouncing over the collar of her uniform shirt while I stood there, mouth gaping with unspoken platitudes, a pile of laundry in my aching arms and regret in my equally sore heart.

Well, damn it.

I trudged across the yard, bypassing Mom and Daisy who let me go with confused looks on their faces. I'd deal with the explanation for both of them later. For now, I had beds to make up and no way was I using the new sheets and towels I'd bought for next door on the likes of Grace and Philip. They were lucky I had questions to ask them, or they'd be sleeping in the yard.

Grace waited in the hallway like I was some kind of servant as I made up her bed, the entirety of our conversation her grunting at me like I'd barely fulfilled her expectations before she slammed the door in my face. She better not have damaged the wood, or she'd be paying for it.

When I climbed the stairs to Philip's room, I paused outside his closed door at the sound of his voice speaking low but clearly upset. Now, it's not that I was in the habit of eavesdropping on my guests—I said my guests. I'm well aware I'm a snoop otherwise—but his situation wasn't exactly typical, so I wasn't feeling particularly guilty when I paused at the keyhole to listen.

"—not my fault he's dead," he snarled. He had to be on the phone because I didn't hear the response despite the fact he paused, then spoke a moment later. "How should I know? Don't blame me. I'm here doing my damned job, the job you hired me to do." Well now, wasn't that interesting? What job was he referring to? He must have drifted closer to the door because I could now hear faint yelling as if whoever he spoke to had reached sufficient volume their tone (if not their words) were audible. "I have it under control. Yes, I'll handle it." Another pause. "Seriously, this is good for us. Trust me."

Whoever it was finished their conversation abruptly because he swore softly. I straightened just as the door whooshed open, Philip staring down at me in surprise to find me there. It took a moment of both of us standing very still, shock wearing to anger on his face, my instinctual guilt over getting caught spinning into my own version of temper before he grabbed the sheets and towels from my hands and slammed the door in my face much as Grace had.

Seriously. Neither of them had any respect for wood.

CHAPTER TWENTY-ONE

I was at the back door when I heard Philip leave and immediately turned to retrace my steps. Grace poked her nose out but retreated instantly while I returned upstairs. Hey, I had to make the bed, right? No way he was ruining my new mattress. Of course, the chance to poke around a bit? Hard to pass up.

My luck he hadn't unpacked at all and there was nothing to see, really. I knew better than to be so blatant as to go through his things, though by the time I was done making the bed and setting up the towels in the bathroom the temptation to rifle through his suitcase was so powerful I was shaking. Instead, I forced myself to leave the bedroom and lock the door firmly behind me, proud of myself for doing the right thing while my inner snoop sulked in the corner.

When I finally emerged from the annex, heading back to Petunia's with a serious case of frustration and the need to upend everything that happened on Mom or Daisy or both before I exploded, I practically stumbled on Grace. She sat on the back step, weeping softly, rocking as she hugged herself in the morning sunlight.

Now, I'm not made of stone, nor am I one to hold grudges when emotions are involved. Sure, I have a bad temper and if you piss me off, I can have a bit of a meltdown. But seeing her sitting there crying hit all the feels I wished they hadn't, triggering the memory that not so long ago the man she'd been sharing a room with died tragically at the hands of someone who murdered him.

I sat slowly next to her, not touching her—my empathy only went so far—and not saying anything, just offering her companionship while she grieved. Grace wiped at her face before blinking at me, a sad smile erasing the last of her arrogance and showing me the sorrowful woman beneath. She wasn't traditionally attractive, not that those kinds of things mattered, but in that moment, she seemed lovely to me and I softened the rest of the way while she sadly patted my hand.

"I'm sorry," she whispered, still choked up. "How I treated you, dear. So terrible of me. It's just been such a shock."

I nodded, squeezed her hand back. "Can I offer you tea?"

Grace's eyes filled with tears again. "Thank you,

that would be wonderful."

I seated her at one of the garden tables and hurried back to Petunia's. Mom's arched eyebrows at my request was her only response, though I was positive she had a million questions. Instead of filling her in just yet, I relieved her of the tea service she prepared, Clara already gone, apparently, leaving this job to Mom—and hurried back to Grace, hoping the old woman hadn't recovered from her weeping fit just yet.

Oh, Fee. You're a horrible, horrible person.

Fortunately or not, depending on your point of view, Grace was still in the throes of misery when I rejoined her. I offered some tissues I'd nabbed from the kitchen on my way out before serving tea, two lumps of sugar and a dollop of cream satisfying her while she spoke.

"He was such a lovely, passionate person," she gushed, helping herself to two cookies in quick succession, the crumbs cascading into her lap though she didn't seem to notice. I rested my chin on my folded hands and nodded encouragement for her to go on. "So driven by his beliefs and so committed to the cause." She exhaled a few bits of confection, the particles landing in her tea as she slurped up a mouthful. China rattled when she settled the cup into the saucer. "His death is a huge loss to the community." Her lower lip trembled. "However will we go on without him?"

"You were together a long time?" I pushed the cookies toward her and watched her devour a third in two bites, followed by a long swig of tea I topped up without a word as she blushed a bit, though with a faintly naughty expression that added youth to her face.

"Well, I'm just old, dear, not dead." She sighed then, fourth cookie limp in her fingers before she jammed it into her mouth and chewed absently. "I stood by his side for years. I just can't believe it ended this way." She sobbed once, spilling tea down the front of her vest. For the first time, I felt actual guilt over my attitude and helped her dab at the moisture with a handful of napkins before she caught my wrist and stared into my eyes, hers full of grief. "I honestly don't know what I'm going to do without him," she said, voice shaking. "He was everything to me. And our dream… I'm so worried it dies with him."

"I'm sure you'll find a way to keep going," I said. "There are new, young voices that want to help, right? Like Philip?"

Grace shook her head, looked down at the napkins crushed into a wad in her lap, fingering a fresh, dirty tear in the corner of one of the pockets of her khaki vest like picking at a scab. "I fear the protesting youth don't have the kind of fire that men like Lewis possess," she said. "I wish I knew more about that young man. But he was a friend of Lewis's, so I trust him to carry on, I suppose." She choked again, the napkins now pressed grotesquely to her mouth, the clump so big the white ends trailed out between her fingers like the legs of a bloated bug she squashed without mercy. "I've been at Lewis's side for every single protest, sick and healthy, rain and shine, for the last fifteen years." Her hand fell once again, the muffled words clear with the motion. "Everything I knew and believed and loved is gone."

I patted her hand, offering her another cookie which she accepted. I should have brought more, apparently. "What made you think there were woodpeckers, Grace?"

She shrugged that off immediately, ,though she looked suddenly uncomfortable. "That was Lewis's department."

Okay then. "There seemed to be a lot of media," I said. "Does that happen at every protest?"

She nodded then with renewed enthusiasm. "Oh, yes," she gushed. "The media love Lewis." Her face crumbled then as if she understood she used present tense when past was now appropriate.

"Are they usually supportive?" I hesitated before blurting the rest. "Like Fleur King, for example?"

Everything in Grace shifted. Her grief dried up in a heartbeat, the softer side of her vanishing like it had never been even as she threw down the wad of napkins on the ground and pushed herself to her sturdy feet, the heels of her heavy shoes digging into the soft ground of the garden beneath her.

"That horrible creature," she snapped. "Maybe your sheriff should investigate her for Lewis's murder."

And before I could stop her and ask her what she was talking about, get any information from her about Fleur's investigation, Grace spun and stomped off. And didn't she slam the back door to the annex?

Jared was right about the added expense being worth it in the end when he made the suggestion for the hardware. I'd be springing for soft hinges after all. Meanwhile, it was time for some serious investigation into this mess on my own.

CHAPTER TWENTY-TWO

As it turned out there was no time for an internet search. From the moment I returned to Petunia's until dinner service ended it seemed like there was one fire to put out after another, from a freak plumbing issue in room nine to failure of delivery of our bread order from French's Handmade Bakery I had to handle personally to a misplaced reservation that left me pulling my hair out until Jill and Robert finally finished their examination of Lewis's room. Not to mention Clara's unexpected decision to back out entirely with a simple, "I quit," phone call leaving me growling.

I exhaled as I stacked the last plate into the dishwasher and turned it on, Daisy sagging over the counter, Mom beside her, the two of them looking about as wiped out as I felt. The other staff had already gone home, just as well. I think my meanness trend hadn't eased up though I wasn't sure why telling Suzie/Megan/Chloe/Whoever to hustle her butt was enough cause to make the kid cry.

Okay, so maybe I was a little harsh. And the reason Clara quit. Whoops.

"Fiona Fleming," Mom finally said, faint frown between her eyes. "Sit yourself down and tell us who put a bee in your bonnet and why it is exactly you've been running around all day like the world kicked your puppy."

Petunia whined softly at her feet as if thinking Mom was talking about her. I took a second to fetch a bag of frozen banana slices from the freezer and sighed as I sat down, handing over the first of a carefully measured dozen to the drooling pug. She hopped from foot to foot as I took my time dolling out her treat and shared with Mom and Daisy what happened.

By the time I was done, they were both shaking their heads.

"Aundrea called earlier," Mom said. "Jared was released after Philip. I hope that boy has the sense to leave well enough alone. Though she didn't know what the problem was in the first place and he's not talking."

Another mystery to sort out. I met Daisy's eyes, winced. "I'm sorry about making Chloe cry." Gave Petunia an extra slice of banana like I could make up for the mess ahead. "And Clara quit."

She looked confused a moment, then laughed.

"Rebecca," she said while I groaned and decided to stop trying. "I handled it."

Right. Rebecca. Bless her.

"As for Clara," Mom sniffed, "that wasn't you. It was me." Phew, good to know. "She was using boxed stuffing, Fiona. *Boxed.* Honestly."

A deeply immoral and likely illegal act in my mother's eyes. From the grin on Daisy's face, she wasn't upset with the loss and, frankly, neither was I and since I'd asked Mom to handle the food side of things...

Okay then.

I sent the two women home for the night, hugging them both with giant thanks, accepting Daisy's offer to trot over to the annex to check on Grace and Philip before she left. I really should have found someone to monitor the other house, but they could just fend for themselves for the night. For now, I sat down behind the computer in the foyer for some website searching with a long list of names I found I just had to know more about.

Two hours and a headache later and I sat back from the notes I'd taken between looking up and smiling and chatting with guests and my nosy investigations. Likely the cause of my headache, but oh well, I had dug up enough to make me even more curious than I had been before I started. Crew would be ecstatic.

Fleur, it turned out, was a bit of a name for herself as well, the recipient of a number of awards not only here in the U.S. but around the world, digging into the kind of global environmental issues that made reporters famous. Recently, her coverage of an oil spill off the coast to a fracking installation that locals claimed caused earthquakes and undrinkable water had shown a shift in pattern, Fleur's passion for covering stories to do with Mother Earth driving her career. At least she seemed legit enough, though I wondered at her sudden turn to domestic issues and why she'd stopped traveling to cover small stories like this one.

Maybe not so small after all?

As for Lewis and Grace, their own story was about as public as it could get. Just typing his name into the search engine gave me so many hits my head swam. No issue was too small, no protest too out of touch with reality. If he wasn't supporting a tiny community in northern Michigan to preserve a habitat for a beetle that actually devoured healthy crops, he was waxing poetic about endangered slugs that as far as I could tell no one gave a damn about until he brought them up. And chaining himself to trees? His favorite pastime.

And there was Grace, at his side, just as she'd said, the two of them aging slowly over the course of the images I perused, fifteen years together unfolding as the internet disgorged their track record in a collection of news articles, blogs and photographs that told a tale of a pair of passionate people who really needed to get lives already. Yes, I was all for saving the environment and everything, but when an entire elementary school was in tears because Lewis

Brown called the children murderers thanks to the discovery of a rare butterfly colony they'd been raising in captivity?

Seriously.

As for Philip, he seemed to kind of appear out of nowhere on the protestor scene, though I did find reference to him at the University of Vermont. Surprisingly, considering not one of the three mentioned knowing him, it turned out he graduated the same year as Jared, Carmen and Aiden. Unlike *Zip It!*'s young owners, though there was nothing environmental in his studies. In fact, he'd departed that fine institution with a degree in business. So, what was he doing chasing endangered woodpecker sightings in a zip line park in Reading?

The message boards for the more outspoken protest organizations made mention of him and his newcomer status, but no one seemed to know who he was or why he'd been recruited. Vetting from Lewis smoothed things over quickly, however. The outpouring of grief on those same sites, all fresh, felt genuine and made my guilt resurface fast enough I clicked off to other destinations rather than lingering. Crew would be digging into Lewis. I was more interested in the outliers at the moment.

Aiden and Carmen, on the other hand, both took environmental studies, the pair of them side by side in photos on their department's website, their college profiles professing they pretty much fell in love day one and had been together the entire duration of their stay. And there, smiling next to them? Jared

Wilkins himself, the third wheel of their particularly wobbly cart, though he never looked out of place. So, best friends, then?

I was sad not to see Alicia among them and wondered again about Jared's history with Carmen. Rather than doubt the young man I adored, I switched tactics and dove back into the protest movement involvement in *Zip It!*.

It took me about a minute to uncover the first claim of the woodpecker sighting, but no one seemed to take ownership of the initial instance. Pretty flimsy evidence, if you asked me. Considering the county cleared the park, it felt about as iffy as the Reading hoard showing up anywhere near this town. Then again, if Grandmother Iris wasn't leading me on a wild pirate chase, maybe I was as wrong about the woodpeckers as the debunking treasure hunters were about the hoard's existence.

Didn't matter now. The damage to Carmen and Aiden's business was done. And Lewis Brown was dead. Though whether over the little birds or some other issue I had yet to understand, it didn't really matter at the moment.

What did matter? Someone deliberately tried to shut down *Zip It!*. But why? A grudge against Aiden and Carmen? I couldn't find anything negative about the two, not on their unprotected social media—honestly, did they not understand the privacy settings were there for their protection?—nor on the actual protestor message boards or anywhere else. They seemed pretty universally liked until the woodpecker thing came up. And even some of the more prominent protestors on the more common sites came across as hesitant to jump on board, even with Lewis leading the charge.

So if the big names of the environmentally-minded weren't sold, what was up?

I really needed to sit tight. I couldn't just up and leave Petunia's. The house was full, and I had guests to care for. But I had questions and when I called the ranger's station, no one answered. I frowned at my computer, tapping my fingers on the keys, humming softly in agitation. Just as my father walked through the front door.

I beamed at him, hurried to hug him. Dad hugged me back, smiling, kissing my forehead. Before he could say a word, I grabbed for my jacket and Petunia's lead, the pug practically huffing her excitement at the sight.

"I need to run out," I said. "Can you watch things for a half-hour?"

Dad looked instantly disappointed, but shrugged out of his own coat, hanging it over the back of the stool at the computer. "Sure, sweetheart," he said. "But I want to talk to you when you get back."

Hmmm. About Mom, maybe? He didn't seem upset, so it might have been.

"I promise," I said, kissing his cheek before bending to slip Petunia's chubby body into the padded pink straps, a recent gift from Daisy. "I'll be right back!"

It was just a short drive to the station, Petunia

perched on the seat next to me, panting her happy contentment into the darkness that had fallen over my hometown.

"We'll be quick," I said to her while she grinned at me like I was the only one judging me for running away from my responsibilities again for the sake of a mystery. "See, this is why I need Mom and Daisy as partners, right? I'm terribly irresponsible."

Petunia meowed one of her squeaky yawns that was more cat than dog and kept grinning.

I pulled into the ranger's station at the same time Matt was climbing into his truck. He seemed surprised to see me, waved as I exited my car, Petunia hopping down to the graveled ground with a grunt. She sat on my foot and panted up at the handsome ranger who crouched to scratch her ears, the subsequent groans of her delight almost embarrassing.

"Sorry to bother you," I said, "but I had a few questions, and I couldn't reach you."

"I was out patrolling," he said, standing up to tower over me at his full height. He was almost as tall as Crew, not quite as broad through the shoulders. Wait, why was I noticing anyway? Comparing? Sheesh, get a grip, Fleming. "What did you need?"

He seemed perfectly normal and not at all staring at me like he had at Petunia's earlier, so I had to have imagined the rather embarrassing things I thought about him. Like the fact I suspected he was into me even though I'd never noticed. Wow, I really was full of myself. Poor guy. Good thing I hadn't said anything and totally humiliated myself.

Instead, I grinned quickly to hide the flinch of my overreaction about my own assumptions. "I was wondering about the woodpeckers."

He shrugged, smiled easily back. "Not sure what to tell you," he said. "They aren't even supposed to be in this area anymore. They've been extinct in our region for years. They still have habitat in the southeast, so seeing them this far north is kind of a big deal."

From the tone of his voice, he wasn't buying it. "You're not convinced?"

Matt dug his hands into the back pockets of his jeans. Only then did I notice he'd changed out of his uniform, only his government-issue jacket and the gun on his hip indication he was, in effect, a police officer as well as a park ranger. I was so used to seeing him in his uniform it felt odd to remember he was a person, too.

I was such a weirdo.

"I'm not," he said. "I did my master's program in indigenous birds in this area. I have to say, it would be a miracle to find them here, not just because they've been gone so long, but because of the change in habitat." He sounded competently confident enough to me. "Even an attempt to reintroduce a family to New Hampshire five years ago failed. So, how they'd accomplish it on their own... well, nature is funny. But not that funny."

"I had no idea you had a master's," I said. Not that I was easily impressed, but I'd never considered him particularly scholarly.

He winked. "I guess neither of us is just a pretty face."

Um, awkward, but in a rather adorable way. I giggled despite myself. "I guess not." I shivered then in the breeze that picked up, Petunia whining softly while I huddled a moment inside my jacket, wishing I'd brought a warmer one. "So, you think this was a setup?"

Matt stared at me a long moment before taking a step forward, arms going around me. I froze in place as he hugged me, chin on the top of my head. "Pretty sure that's the case," he said, voice deep and husky all of a sudden while my heart stopped.

At the exact second a sheriff's department cruiser pulled into the parking lot.

CHAPTER TWENTY-THREE

I have no idea why I flinched away from Matt. It was obvious he was just trying to help me stay warm while he answered my questions, right? Right? Just my luck, it was Robert who climbed out, grinning at the two of us like he'd uncovered some grand conspiracy, beady eyes darting back and forth between us while he sauntered closer, that ridiculous mustache twitching.

"Fanny," he said. "Matt. Nice evening for a rendezvous."

Oh, whatever, you icky creepzilla. "What do you want, Robert?"

He shrugged then, winked lewdly at Matt who looked about as uncomfortable as I did, scowling like he wanted to punch Robert. I wouldn't have argued except the first hit was mine.

"Crew's looking for you," he said to the ranger. His gaze flickered to me. "I'll let him know the two of you are otherwise occupied."

"Fee was just cold," Matt said, sounding sullen enough I groaned inwardly. Damn it, I was right earlier, he was into me. Had I somehow given him the impression I felt the same about him? This had horrifying potential to turn into something I really didn't have time to deal with right now.

"Right," Robert drawled, hands on hips, pushing his pelvis toward me in a truly disgusting gesture that almost got him killed then and there, I swear. "Cold. Gotcha."

I swiftly closed the distance between myself and my cousin, jabbing him so hard in his beer gut he grunted and backed off, his nasty smile turning to a scowl of his own.

"Get your sick and twisted mind out of the gutter for once," I snarled. "And mind your own damned business."

Robert stuck that ugly mustache in my face, his narrowed eyes locked on mine. "We'll just see what Crew thinks about your little cuddle session, Fanny." He turned his back on me like we were in high school, and he could actually impact my life with a piece of trash talk garbage gossip. Climbed into his cruiser with an index finger jabbed first at Matt then me which he used to pull an imaginary trigger before laughing and slamming his door, peeling off, gravel spraying out behind him.

Well, damn it. High school it was, I guess. I spun

on Matt, heat in my cheeks, no longer needing a warmer coat, and frowned at him while he blushed in the glaring light over the ranger station.

"Tell me you weren't hitting on me," I said.

He stuttered and stammered long enough, not meeting my gaze, I put an end to the lack of conversation by sighing heavily and tugging on Petunia's leash, leading her to my car. His footfalls ended with his hand on my arm, and he spun me around, the pug already hopped up into the driver's seat. I looked into Matt's eyes, wished I didn't see the longing there, the unrequited emotions that I really wasn't expecting, and knew I had to let him down gently before this went any further.

But whatever I had to say to him, I didn't get the chance. Instead of waiting to be let down, Matt turned and hurried to the station door, disappearing inside. I stood there for a long moment, getting cold all over again, wishing I had the courage to go after him and just put an end to it once and for all, but unable to muster the nerve.

Instead, Petunia whining finally she was as chilled as I was, I pushed her over into the passenger's seat and joined her, cranking the heat once we were on the road, groaning over what Robert might say to Crew and wishing I didn't care. Wanting to believe the sheriff I was rapidly falling for wouldn't take the childish word of my ridiculous cousin I'd been inappropriate with another guy while wavering into frustration that I shouldn't have to explain myself anyway since I didn't do anything wrong.

Fun drive home, let me tell you. I was in such a lather of anxiety and annoyance by the time I reached downtown I drove directly to the sheriff's office to talk to Crew personally. When I didn't spot his truck, I instead cruised past his house, embarrassed to find he wasn't home and that I was actually stalking him now. On impulse, feeling bad for leaving Dad alone at Petunia's but needing to meet this head on, I drove out to the only other place I was sure he'd be.

Crew's truck was parked near the entrance of *Zip It!* but unfortunately so was Robert's cruiser. There was no sign of Matt's ranger vehicle, though, so I had that going for me. Knowing it was a disaster waiting to happen and wondering what the hell I was actually doing there in the first place, I climbed out of the car, Petunia hopping down gamely to join me, free of complaint, as I leaped over the barricade, the pug weaving easily under the gate, and entered the park.

I was in such a hurry to reach Crew before Robert could pull his jerkish act and cause the sheriff any kind of discomfort—not to mention my discomfort, thanks—I failed to notice the shortcut I took past the main entry building led me into a small stand of bushes. And that, as I passed into the center of the collection of thick shrubbery, I wasn't alone.

Not that the pair in the middle of said foliage noticed me, though it was clear from the light shining through the leaves the guy Carmen was kissing rather vigorously wasn't Aiden. Nope, not even close. And when he turned his head for better traction on her lips? Well, the reason for Jared's animosity toward

Philip became fairly clear.

The fact I'd caught the protestor and the park owner kissing wasn't lost on me. However, their embrace, unlike me and Matt? Kind of hard to misconstrue their make-out session as anything but exactly what it was.

CHAPTER TWENTY-FOUR

Carmen noticed me first, while I stared at them in shock and tried to figure out what to do, wishing I was anywhere but there at that moment. She jerked herself free of Philip, backing away until she impacted one of the bushes which she then leaped away from, putting herself back in his reach as terror crossed her face. She flushed deeply, Philip meeting my eyes a moment as his own flared with shock, then barely contained anger.

He could be as mad at me as he wanted, but I wasn't the one making out with the enemy.

"It's not what it looks like." Carmen's hurried attempt at a blatant lie silenced her without me having to say a word.

"I personally couldn't care less." I stepped aside while Philip left in a rush without a word to the girl he'd just been kissing, disappearing toward the entry while Carmen watched him go, hugging herself as he did, despair on her face. "None of my business. Unless, of course, your affair impacts Lewis Brown's death."

Carmen's face crumpled, tears tracking down her cheeks. "We had nothing to do with that," she said. "Philip and I... we have history. That's all. I wasn't expecting to see him here."

"Bet Aiden wasn't happy to see him either," I said. "Jared certainly took exception."

Carmen sniffed, wiping her nose on the cuff of her hoodie, *Zip It!* written across the front in giant white letters. I had one just like it, thanks to Lewis's death. "Jared needs to mind his own business. I didn't ask for him to interfere."

"Likely he thought he was defending his friend," I said, not saying which friend that might be and wondering if she knew I referred to Aiden far more than her. Looked like she'd made her choices, hadn't she?

She shook her head, lips a tight line. "Philip wasn't supposed to be here," she said. "I told him I never wanted to see him again." Carmen finally met my eyes. "I committed to Aiden, Fee, I swear it."

Good for her. "You must have figured he'd show," I said, "considering he's part of Lewis Brown's little posse."

She seemed to choke on that a moment. "That's just it," she said, voice shaking, "I had no idea he'd started this nonsense." Her lower lip settled as she drew a deep breath and seemed to get control of herself. "He works for a development company, the Blackstone Corporation. They buy up land in emerging areas, turn them into tourist locations. He shouldn't be associating with protestors. He could lose his job."

Interesting and fired off a bunch of warning bells in my head. "Emerging areas like this one?"

Carmen blinked at me. "Yes," she whispered. Shook herself, looked around. "Exactly like this one."

I needed to talk to Jared. Had this Blackstone Corporation approached him about purchasing the land *Zip It!* was built on? My thoughts then zinged to Olivia. If so, did the mayor know about their interest? Or was I grasping at straws of things that had nothing to do with one another? Philip was talking to someone in the annex, though. Someone who wanted him to handle a situation that he said was to their advantage. Was he only playing at being a protestor? But why would someone like Lewis Black trust an employee of a development company?

So many questions. Meanwhile, Carmen lunged for me, grasped my hand, Petunia whining as the young woman came too close for comfort.

"You can't tell Aiden." Desperation lived in her dark eyes and for the second time in a very short period, I thought about high school and all the drama that really shouldn't exist for me in the beginning of my third decade on this planet. "Please, Fee, I'm begging you. He'll never get over it."

I sighed, nodded. "It's not my place to tell your boyfriend you're not as in love with him as you thought you were." Nice try to guilt the girl into confessing on her own. I was pretty sure it wouldn't work and from the flinch she gave me, her retreat, I knew I did little but add to her already weighty regrets. I'd lived through cheating, had left the guy I'd committed a large chunk of my life to, so I had very little patience with infidelity. And realized then that was why I felt so anxious about Matt, about what Robert might tell Crew. Because that wasn't me and never would be.

Argh. I needed to talk to the sheriff.

"I know he's a mistake," Carmen whispered then like I was some kind of confessor she needed to empty herself to. "I love Aiden. But I can't help myself. Whenever Philip's around, I just…" Okay, maybe I felt a bit of sympathy, but not much. What would happen if my ex, Ryan, showed up? I thought about it for about half a second before snorting to myself. I'd kick him in the privates, that's what. But as I stood there and watched Carmen cry, wiping at more tears with her sleeves, I let go of the animosity I felt for my old boyfriend and did my best not to judge her.

"Where were you when Lewis was killed?" He wasn't a large man, so stringing him up after choking him might have been within Carmen's ability. After all, she was an athlete, strong for her size.

She sniffed, nodded. "I was with a group of media," she said, "showing them the harnesses, how

174

we put safety first." She shrugged. "I was on camera the whole time." Pretty solid alibi. Except she wasn't, was she?

"Crew and I saw you remember," I said. "Chasing Philip." Had she been going after him to confront him for showing up or were they entangled in an embrace when Lewis died?

She flinched. "The sheriff cleared me," she said.

Fine, if Crew said so. But I wasn't so willing to let her off the hook. "And Aiden?" I waited, watched, saw her flinch.

"I don't know," she whispered. "I don't remember seeing him until after I ran to the last line. He was up the tree by the time I got there, letting the winch down." Was that fear on her face?

"Do you think Aiden could have killed Lewis over the park?" I wasn't so sure, but she knew him better than anyone, or likely thought she did. Considering he didn't know her that well if he hadn't acted on the Philip thing? Maybe neither of them was as in tune with the other as they could have been. Still, her answer could be telling.

"I don't know," she said. "He has a temper."

"And Philip?" I'd seen him prior to the murder. He'd seemed out of sorts. Because Carmen was chasing him or because he'd just killed Lewis?

Another pause. "I'm not sure about him either," she said. "I spotted him in the crowd, but I didn't get to talk to him until after." She flushed because talking likely wasn't a big part of their conversation, was it? But explained why she was running after him.

"But I'm less worried about Aiden or Philip and more about…" she trailed off, shook her head, looked away. "Never mind. I didn't say anything."

"About who?" I prodded gently, waited again, Petunia licking her chops audibly in the silence that followed.

"Jared," Carmen said. Then shook herself as if she couldn't bear the thought. "I'm worried about Jared."

She did not just throw him under the bus. I wanted to call her on it but Carmen was done. She turned in the opposite direction Philip went, heading for the front of the entrance building, leaving me alone in the bushes, fuming and annoyed.

The sound of a truck starting up spun me around. I headed back to the parking lot in time to see Crew pulling away, Robert following him in his cruiser and scowled at their departing taillights. The sheriff must have seen my car there. Why didn't he wait?

Frustrated and now even more worried, I headed home with questions and arguments at war in my mind.

CHAPTER TWENTY-FIVE

I was still thinking when I entered the foyer of Petunia's to find Dad waiting for me, hunched over the keyboard of my computer. The perfect person to have this conversation with. But the moment I set foot in the entry, Dad leaped to his feet and grabbed for his coat, eyes sparkling.

"Glad you're back," he said. "Feel like going out again?"

"And leave who to watch Petunia's?" I unhooked my pug from her harness, startled to find Mom emerging from the kitchen with a grim look on her face.

"Just go with your father," she said. "You'd better hurry or you'll miss it."

I frowned up at Dad who seemed more excited than concerned, despite Mom's attitude. Were they talking again? He didn't appear uncomfortable with her presence, so maybe they'd had the conversation they needed to in order to salve their wounds. More other people's lives unfolding without me. How dared they when they knew I needed in on every detail?

Regardless, she flapped her hands at me, and Dad took that as an offer to be complicit in his plan on my part because he tugged at my arm and led me outside again in the cool air of early May to his truck.

I climbed inside before asking the obvious. "Where are we going exactly?"

Dad winked, grinning. "Town meeting," he said. "Going to be a hoot."

Um, my father's sense of humor sometimes left a lot to be desired. "As in someone's going to get hurt?"

Dad shrugged, firing up the engine and pulling away from the curb. "We'll see, I guess."

Great. Just freaking great.

"Dad," I said, "are you working on anything related to the murder of Lewis Brown?"

He didn't answer right away so that was a resounding yes.

"What do you know about Philip Davis?" Another bout of telling silence. "He works for a company called—"

"Blackstone," Dad grunted. "Yeah. I know."

"Have they been trying to buy the property that *Zip It!* was built on?" I watched his face carefully in the flare of the streetlights as Dad found a spot and parked a block from town hall. He turned and met my eyes, his unreadable.

"I wouldn't know about that, Fee," he said. And winked.

Sigh.

No time for further questions, not while Dad was leaping out of the truck and heading for the front doors of the hall, leaving me to hurry after him, catching him in time to scoot through the door and into the main foyer of the building. It was packed with people, some of them flustered, most of them bemused as if this meeting came as a surprise to everyone.

"Was a last-minute kind of thing," Dad muttered to me with a barely concealed grin. "I think it was supposed to happen quiet-like."

"Dad," I said, dragging out the word. "Did you...?"

He blinked at me, all innocence. "I might have sent out a few emails when I found out," he said. "You know, just as a heads up for the good townsfolk of Reading."

Snort. Wait, he'd sent those emails from my computer, hadn't he? Oooh. Dads. "You're turning into a troublemaker," I said.

Dad nudged me with one elbow. "I've always been a troublemaker," he whispered. "Don't tell your mother."

Why did that make me want to giggle hysterically?

I joined the influx of people heading for the council chamber, caught the flare of anger on Olivia's face, the smug self-satisfaction from Geoffrey, the startled look from the rest of the council. Was the Patterson connection Dad's source? Or was Geoffrey somehow feeding info to my father? And did Dad know about it? Didn't matter at the moment, but I'd be getting to the bottom of it because no way was that smarmy creep manipulating my dad. Not that he needed my protection, mind you, but I still felt as protective of him as he likely felt about me.

Flemings.

I took a seat in the gallery, the bulk of the townsfolk huddled in around the sitting council, the rest crowding the door and listening in as Olivia called the meeting to order. She seemed more flustered than I'd ever seen her, stumbling and at a loss for a bit, something Geoffrey took advantage of as she fumbled for words while shuffling paper in front of her.

"Thank you for joining us in a timely fashion, fine folk of Reading," he said, drawing out a laugh from everyone as Olivia turned and glared at him. "I love how there are so few secrets in our delightful burg."

"I call this emergency meeting to order," she snapped at him. "Thanks to the devastating death of an internationally famous activist, we've been inundated with media, and it's come to my attention that some of the sitting council have been talking with journalists out of turn."

"Heaven forbid we talk out of turn," Geoffrey said, raising another group chuckle. Dad sat eager and tense next to me, his eyes never leaving the gathered council. What was he after?

Olivia seemed flustered by the amusement. "This was meant to be a private meeting."

"Which goes against the mandate of our town council," Geoffrey said loud enough he meant it to be heard. "Am I right, good people of Reading?"

Mutters of agreement met his statement. I personally didn't give a crap, but something important was going on here, clearly, or Dad wouldn't be involved.

"She's faltering," he whispered to me as if reading my mind. "This might be her death song, Fee. The content of the conversation doesn't matter. It's the end result. Watch." He didn't appear happy about it, just focused, so I did as he said and paid attention.

Frankly, it was sad to observe. Like Dad said, the actual topic wasn't particularly relevant or important, as far as I was concerned. And I had little doubt Olivia had called meetings of this nature without issue in the past, likely holding a great deal of behind-the-scenes conversations that went against town laws to get jobs done. It felt to me like she wasn't prepared to be challenged, or that she'd expected an easy go of it. Instead, as she attempted to wrangle the council under her thumb, Geoffrey systematically dismantled any kind of control she might have had with a few well-placed comments that had the crowd—and the gathering of councilors—laughing at her.

I don't remember the actual contents of the meeting. I was so tied into the emotional toll it took on Olivia, the visible degradation of her downfall, I barely heard a word she said, what Geoffrey said. Instead, the derisive giggling and amusement at her increasingly desperate need to pull things together horrified and disturbed me. Even Dad seemed to have had enough by the time Olivia raised her gavel and shut the whole thing down, his face twisted into something resembling regret.

I exhaled as the hammer fell and the crowd around me burst into chatter, quickly emptying the council chamber. I didn't know what was decided on the topic at hand, but it was clear the other item in question—Olivia's fitness for leadership—was apparently well on the way to an endgame.

Dad grasped my hand and held me in place until most of the people were gone. Only when the council started to break up did he rise to his feet and let me go. I followed him when he approached the council members who now talked among themselves, appearing to distance their physical bodies from Olivia who shuffled papers and stared at the table in front of her like doing so would save her from losing her place as mayor. A horrible feeling of loss washed through me and it was a huge battle to keep from rushing to her side and telling them all to go to hell.

Ungrateful jerks.

I looked up to find Dad talking to Geoffrey at the exact moment the Patterson puppet gave me a blatant up and down with his vulture-like gaze. So gross. Dad noticed, scowled, said something that caught the accountant's attention and only then did

Geoffrey seem to realize who he was talking to. I avoided them both, huddled inside my light jacket, wishing I'd stayed home instead of following Dad here.

It wasn't until Olivia stood up I headed for her, ignoring the rest of the council, joining her as she circled the desk, grasping for her elbow. She paused when I did, blinked as if she only then noticed I was there before shuddering to a halt and forcing a smile.

"Fiona." She swallowed, straightened her shoulders, that kind of too stiff falseness to her body that told me she knew she was on the brink if not already sliding down the hill at a rapidly increasing rate. "How lovely to see you."

"Olivia." I could have asked her about tonight, about how to help and saw rejection in her eyes. Decided to let her have this moment of denial. I instead asked a question burning in the back of my mind. "Did Blackstone Corporation make an offer on the *Zip It!* property before Jared developed it?"

She started like she'd expected something far different, frowning a little. "I can't divulge anything like that, Fee," she said. "That's town business." She hesitated a moment before pulling her arm free. "Now, if you'll excuse me, I have things to see to." She marched off alone, a solitary figure in a business suit and polished bob, her pumps clicking on the stone floor. I almost went after her, but Terri's appearance at my side stopped me.

"Blackstone did make an offer," the young flower shop owner said, nodding, her dark hair falling over one shoulder, voice low and faintly accented. "The land belonged to Olivia's grandfather originally."

How interesting. "How did Jared acquire it then?"

"He bid on it," she said, glancing at the other council members, clearly aware of the fact she wasn't supposed to talk about it but not seeming to care. "Olivia tried to keep it private, to shut down the bids and let Blackstone win uncontested but Jared found out and his bid won." She shrugged. "All major purchases have to go through council, especially if there are foreign investors. Because Jared's local and his bid was a few thousand higher, she had to sell to him."

Was Olivia in Blackstone's pockets? Why would she sell out Reading to a development corporation? That didn't sound like her unless she was planning something I couldn't bring myself to accept. Olivia couldn't have been selling out our town for profit, could she?

"I think she might have gotten away with it," Terri whispered, "but the Pattersons found out and started throwing their weight around." She glanced sideways at Geoffrey, still talking to Dad. "Honestly, the rest of us wanted the land to stay local, too, so we voted against her."

I nodded absently, mind whirling, still struggling to believe Olivia might hand over the keys to the kingdom like that. She'd been spiraling downward into her desperate need to fulfill her own private agenda, though. Was it beyond her to profit from such a deal if she knew she was on her way out? I hated to think so, but she was as human as the next person.

"All I know," Terri said, "is she was really upset and even more so about tonight. I've never seen her so rattled."

Nor had I. "Who's in line for mayor if she goes down?" Not that I had to ask.

Terri's lips twisted. "Geoffrey," she said like there was any doubt. "That means the Patterson family. He's married to one of the cousins, in case you didn't know." I didn't. Not just their accountant, then, but family. Even worse. "And I'm not sure I'm comfortable with that, either."

Frankly, neither was I.

"I can't stand him, Fee," she hissed in my ear, leaning closer as Oliver Watters and Sophia Bell walked by us, chatting with their heads down. "But I have to admit, he has impressive ideas. And without a more viable option, I think he's going to end up leading Reading."

Geoffrey Jenkins, owned by the Pattersons, pied piping us on a new path. But to where? And to whose benefit?

CHAPTER TWENTY-SIX

"How much of Reading is now owned by outsiders?" I had never thought to ask, never considered the question before. I was so wrapped up in my own problems, in Petunia's and the annex and murders I'd failed to consider the place where I grew up and now did business might be at some kind of crossroads of its own.

Terri seemed uncomfortable with the question. "Technically, I'm an outsider," she said.

I grasped her hand, shook my head. "You live here," I said as way of an apology. "I mean corporations, business holdings."

Terri seemed to accept the correction. "A bit," she said, "but less than you'd think. The Patterson family lobbies endlessly against it. I think they've been working against Olivia since she took power."

So, they saw Olivia—and the encroachment of control of "their" town—as a threat? Well, I kind of did, too, truth be told. Except, my bottom line kind of relied on it. Did that make me a hypocrite? I guess so. "How much do you know about them, anyway?"

She shrugged. "Not much. Except, if you want to add irony to the story, most of them don't even live here anymore." That elicited a smirk from both of us. "The old matriarch rules from that manor house over the lake but no one ever sees her except the family, from what I hear. And they control all the property on that side of the mountain, so anyone building nearby has been completely cut off." I was aware of that, the emptiness of the land around the manor, only visible from Cutter Lake.

Maybe I needed to take a drive, get lost, pay them a friendly visit...? Now I was just getting sidetracked. Still, this was my town, too.

"Despite their efforts? Fee, I'm nervous." She sighed as she locked eyes with me. "The only reason I'm talking out of turn." Okay, fair enough. Though what she thought I'd do with the information I had no idea. "While the town proper and the immediate area remain under the control of locals, most of the surrounds, anything that's been for sale recently, has been snapped up by outsiders. Mostly holdings, conglomerates with names I've never heard of and that have no digital presence." So, she'd been doing research on her own, good for her. "It's sad, but it's the way things go. At least, that's what I've been told when I've brought it up during meetings." She didn't seem to buy that argument. "I love Reading, Fee. I've lived here for ten years now and despite its flaws, it's home. That goes for Olivia. She might not always have great ideas, but I honestly think she has the best intentions for this town."

My mind went to the Valentine's Day party at the White Valley Ski Lodge, the foreign investors Olivia invited, the drive she'd had to increase our visibility and tourism. "Even with the Blackstone deal?" I waited for her to change her mind, but Terri didn't.

"There's more going on here than we know," she said at last, hands tucking in her pockets, shoulders bowed in the beginnings of misery. "I don't think it's going to end well if Geoffrey and the Pattersons are allowed to take over."

One thing was certain. Olivia's plans for Reading weren't going to unfold further if her reputation's degradation and Geoffrey's growing influence continued as they were. Trouble was, which side should I be on? Sure, he gave me the creeps, but was the family protecting Reading from being consumed by the outside world? Or did Olivia have a plan for us that I couldn't see yet?

"I'm pretty sure the Patterson family is taking a stand against outsiders," Terri said, echoing what I was thinking. "Which means it's likely Geoffrey's pitch to further Reading is a ploy."

"To what end?" I already had my own guess, but I wanted to hear her say it.

She glanced at him, back to me, though I noted his faint scowl as he left Dad at last and headed our way as if only now realizing Terri and I were talking for longer than was polite and social. "To revert Reading back to the way it was," she whispered before hugging me quickly with a fake smile. She left me then, following her fellow councilors while I scowled to myself and stared at the toes of my shoes, worried she was right.

Reading reduced to the old way of things? That would suck. I had an annex to pay for. And the people of this town had invested a lot of time and effort into growth and prosperity. I glared at Geoffrey on the way by, heading for my father, ignoring the accountant with mayoral aspirations as he tried to stop me to talk.

Not tonight, Geoff. If ever. Mind whirling, I grasped Dad's arm and scowled up at him.

"Time to have a conversation," I grumbled and led him out.

Dad wasn't in the mood to chat, though. As soon as we hit the street, he unhooked his arm from mine and kissed the top of my head. "Go home, Fee," he said. "I have some things to look into." He abandoned me then, striding toward his truck and I made no effort to go after him. He knew a lot more than he was saying, that much was evident. But the lights shining through the windows at the *Reading Reader Gazette* distracted me enough I decided to pin Dad down another time in favor of a chat with my favorite newspaperwoman.

If Pamela didn't know what was going on I'd live on frozen banana slices and give Petunia all the crap she wanted for the rest of her snorting, farting existence.

I guess I shouldn't have been surprised to find my friend huddled at her desk with the tall, slim form of Fleur King at her side, the pair whispering over something they instantly shut up about as I let myself into the office and through reception, coming to a halt with a grim nod for both.

"Interesting town meeting you missed just now," I said. "Want me to fill you in?"

Pamela looked startled, Fleur glancing back and forth between us in faint amusement.

"Spill," my friend commanded.

I sat and told her everything, including about Carmen and Philip, though honestly, that part slipped out of me before I could censor myself. From the lack of shock on Pamela's face nothing I told her came as a surprise, while Fleur whistled softly under her breath as I wrapped up.

"You weren't kidding about her," she prodded Pamela in the ribs with a grin. "She's got instincts."

Pamela flashed her a huge smile, far too familiar and conspiratorial I suddenly had suspicions about their history together that had nothing to do with work and everything to do with the kind of relationship that might get my friend into trouble with her fiancé. What was it with my friends this week, the people I encountered? It was like one big conspiracy to betray each other or at least confront temptation in the face of loyalty. Maybe I was just sensitive to it?

There was an awkward moment of silence between them and then Pamela seemed to notice I was there. She twitched like she realized she'd given too much away before speaking. "I know about Blackstone," she said, "and the property grab attempts. That the Pattersons are making their presence known for the first time in a long time." She glanced at Fleur who didn't comment. "I've been working on a story, but Jared's purchase silenced the buy so I kind of stopped investigating." Not to mention her engagement to his mother, maybe, influencing her choice? "Until Fleur showed up, that is."

The lean photojournalist shifted in her seat as if physical motion could shake off her reticence. She finally ey- rolled and grinned at me like she'd made a decision that didn't sit well with her but was out of her hands.

"Fine," she said. "Pam trusts you, I trust you. But this is my scoop and if you toss me to the wolves, I'll make sure you regret it." Um, not scared. I'd almost died a couple of times and the dead bodies I'd found? Piling up at an alarming rate. Besides, I didn't owe her anything, but as long as she wasn't doing anything to hurt the people I cared about I had no problem keeping quiet. "I've seen stories like this one unfolding all around the eastern seaboard and beyond. And it worries me."

"What kind of stories?" I sat back, waited.

"Small towns building themselves up," Fleur said, "finding tourism opportunities, or industry that attracts attention." She spread her long fingers wide, resting them on the thighs of her jeans. "Then, out of nowhere, someone reports an endangered species appearance, an animal or a plant, and the activists appear to shut things down." She glanced at Pamela who didn't comment. "In almost all cases, the disturbance has closed off local efforts to develop and left the surrounding properties open to purchase at highly reduced rates."

"Big corporations—like Blackstone—come in with specialists who debunk the sightings," Pamela went on, taking over the story while Fleur exhaled and stared at her splayed fingers as if they offended her. "The land is so cheap at that point, the industry and tourism efforts crushed, they buy up everything, promising development."

"Which the locals get," Fleur said, "in the form of clearcutting or fracking or factory farming, that slowly devour the town and become the major employer. They can then drive down wages on the premise of creating jobs. They strip the area of useful resources before they move on to the next location. Meanwhile, the towns that are at the core of the process die because the locals move away thanks to the reduction in their quality of life."

How freaking horrible. "That's what they planned for Reading?" So, Olivia did try to sell us out. My estimation of her plummeted to zero while Pamela spoke.

"The fact Philip is connected to Blackstone means he's at the top of the suspect list." I shook my head then, standing and pacing because I couldn't help myself.

"He's the liaison between the activists and Blackstone," Fleur said. "I've encountered him a time or two before. In fact," she leaned toward the desk, resting both elbows on it, "he's been at every single rally Lewis and that partner of his have organized in the last two years."

So, was Lewis connected to Philip and Blackstone? Was that the reason he was killed? And did Philip kill him despite what he said on the phone?

Pamela exhaled softly, enough to catch my attention while Fleur sat back again, crossing her arms over her narrow chest.

"I shouldn't have stopped investigating," my friend said, sounding sad and frustrated.

"No, you shouldn't," Fleur said, not quite an accusation. "The Pam I knew wouldn't have."

I almost jumped to her defense, but I needn't have bothered.

"Piss off," she snapped at Fleur before grinning.

"You first," Fleur winked back. "Now can you please get your head out of your butt and do your job already? I could use the backup." She met my eyes, hers clear and open. "And yours, if you're in for some further snooping?" I didn't respond right away, but she wasn't done. "See, I'm pretty sure Lewis Brown wasn't a real activist and that he's been working for Blackstone all along. I just need to prove it."

CHAPTER TWENTY-SEVEN

I absorbed that for a moment before asking my next question. "And Grace?" Was she working for the corporation too?

"I don't know," Fleur said. "She was his right hand, though. Surely, she knew everything, at the very least."

Not necessarily, but I didn't say that out loud. After all, Ryan had cheated on me for years and I had no idea. Or did I? No, I refused to accept that I'd known and just didn't want to admit it to myself at the time. His infidelity had come as a total shock. So, it was possible Grace had zero clue about Lewis. But, if she found out, would that be motive for murder?

"I have a money trail," Fleur said, clearly lost in her own thoughts and unaware of where my mind was going. "I've been tracking the cash flow and it's pretty clear Lewis was handsomely compensated for making noise before conveniently disappearing in time for the specialists to clean up the mess he made." Which led me to wonder if anyone in the community of protestors knew Lewis was dirty. Could that be why they were less likely to leap on his bandwagon? Was he suspected by other leaders and motivators and could some of them have wanted him dead for his betrayal?

"We need to tell Crew about this." Fleur's instant groan and scowl told me I was about to have a fight on my hands.

"This is my story," she growled. "It's huge and I'm not going to risk losing it thanks to some bumbling small-town sheriff."

Excuse me very much. "He's far from bumbling," Pamela interjected with that same amused tone and expression she'd had all along. "As a matter of fact, he's former FBI." He was what? I gaped at the newswoman while she winked at me. "Thought you knew? He left the Bureau when his wife died, took this job for goodness knows what reason."

Huh. I had no clue. And my estimation of him jacked up several notches while I wondered how much else there was he hadn't told me about himself.

"Your point being?" Fleur didn't seem mollified. If anything, her back was up further than before. "Once a Fed, always a Fed. He'll turn everything I have over to his friends in suits and my story will be crushed."

"Or," I said, "you could work with him and

scoop the entire thing while he solves it."

She glared at me a moment before sighing. "You're new to this," she said. "So, I'll let you have your innocent illusions for the time being. And I can't stop you from telling him, obviously. But don't ask me to sabotage my own story for the sake of your little town or some dead activist who sold out."

"You might not trust Fee and Crew," Pamela said, one hand on Fleur's arm keeping her from standing and striding away, though the touch looked so light and Fleur's gathered energy so visible in her lean body I wasn't sure how long the other woman could hold her back. "But you know me. You trusted me once. I'm asking you to trust me now."

Fleur's face twisted into denial. "You're not the journalist I knew." But that attack sounded weak, like a shot in the dark while Pamela shrugged and dropped her hand.

"Maybe," she said. "Or I'm less about us versus them and more about getting the job done than I ever was. Up to you, Flower." Fleur eye-rolled at the obvious nickname before flashing a grin at Pamela then me, tight and frustrated.

"Fine," she said, blowing out a gust of air between thin lips. "I'll talk to your Federali sheriff and give him what I have. Happy?"

I was, though Pamela laughed. "Never entirely," she said. "The curse of being a journalist."

Fleur sagged back into her seat, long legs stretching out in front of her. "Just give me tonight to confirm my information." She wasn't looking at my friend but instead stared right at me. "Can I have that much?"

It was impossible not to feel uneasy about agreeing to her request. I needed to talk to Crew myself. Still, if she could uncover the truth and hand it to him on a silver platter, it would go a long way to solving this case and maybe shifting the fate of our town. So, could I in good conscience argue with her?

Well, I *was* a Fleming. I could argue about anything.

"Fee's one of us," Pamela nodded to me, sealing my fate with friendship and a steady stare that made me groan inwardly. "She'll keep her peace until tomorrow. Right, Fee?"

Damn her. "I'll be at the sheriff's station first thing," I said. "You'd both better be there." I didn't wait for confirmation, instead turning and heading for the exit, heart constricting. I needed to see Crew, and not just about this. I wanted to talk to him about what Robert saw, or thought he saw, the intense drive to do so almost too much. But if I went to his house to see him, I'd be spilling everything, I just knew it. While my loyalty to him came first, could I really let Pamela down?

One night. Surely a single sleep wasn't going to make that big a difference.

So, instead of doing the right thing, the smart thing? I went home. To find my father there yet again, waiting for me.

CHAPTER TWENTY-EIGHT

This time Mom had gone, Dad pacing the foyer as I entered. Petunia huffed herself to her feet and came to me in a rush, bumping my shins with her heavy head, whining for attention. Okay, food, not attention. She must have missed her nighttime snack.

Seeing Dad made my traitor heart constrict further. Did he count on the no-contact list? I had told Fleur I wouldn't tell Crew, but did my father qualify, too? I agonized over it as I hurriedly led Petunia into the kitchen, Dad trailing after me.

"Where were you?" He acted like he hadn't abandoned me earlier, driving off in his truck as if I didn't exist. "I needed to talk to you."

"Um, then maybe you should have thought of that before you skipped out." I crouched and handed Petunia her frozen strawberry allotment before scowling at him like he'd cracked his nut. "Right?"

Dad sighed. "Sorry, right. It's been a bit busy." He began pacing again. "I forgot I needed to ask you some questions." He stopped abruptly, frowned like he'd given something away. Which he had.

"You're working for someone, and it's connected to the murder." That much was pretty obvious.

Dad shrugged then, sighing as he sank to a stool and rested his forearms on the counter, leaning in with a faint smile. "I'm getting too old for this, Fee." But the sparkle in his eyes, the growing grin on his face? Totally squashed that line of his. Yeah, sure he was.

"Who are you working for?" I could prod as much as he could. After all, I'd learned from the best.

Evasion, thy name was John Fleming. "Doesn't matter," he said. "Tell me everything."

Since I had my own plans to get as much out of him as possible, I conceded, at least to a point, pausing at the visit I'd just paid to Pamela and Fleur. Dad didn't seem to notice when I stumbled to a halt just short of that, nodding at his hands clasped on the tile counter in front of him.

"I was hired by Philip Davis," Dad said then. "Blackstone."

He was what? "Why?"

"They believe someone planted evidence or created false information to ruin *Zip It!* and shut down the park." Dad shrugged like he wasn't surprised.

"That confirms what I heard," I said before I

could stop myself. Dad's eyes met mine, frown returned.

"From who?"

Whoops. "Doesn't matter. My question is much more important." He didn't seem to think my evasion tactic was worthy, but I rushed on anyway before he could question me further about my source. "Why does Blackstone, a corporation that devours small towns for profit, care about fake environmental protests?"

Dad's frown deepened. "Because they own part of the land around the park," he said. "And they've noted a trend in the past few years, a disturbing trail of false claims against places like Reading where they have interests."

Dad clearly didn't have the entire story and I wasn't in a position to tell him everything. Well, wasn't that craptastic?

"Fiona Fleming," Dad said in his best stern Father knows best voice. "What aren't you telling me?"

Oh, no, he did *not* use that ridiculous attempt at intimidation on me. "Same question back at you, Dad," I said, crossing my arms over my chest the exact instant he sat up and performed the identical action. I imagined we looked pretty similar, two Flemings with scowling expressions facing off over our own stubbornness. Might have been funny if it wasn't so pathetic.

Dad shook his head. "I need to know, Fee."

"So do I." I tilted my head, feeling my rough bun

at the base of my neck shift as it partially let go, my auburn hair falling over my shoulder. Petunia whined softly at me, her bulging eyes shifting to Dad and back again. "You can't trust Philip or Blackstone, Dad."

"I did my due diligence," he said, sounding angry now. "Did you?" His eyes narrowed. "Who's your source, Fee? And what did they tell you?"

No way. Maybe if he didn't try to bully his own daughter I might have caved. But as he sat there, glaring like I was some errant teenager and he was big, bad John Fleming, sheriff and ridiculous town hero or something equally snort worthy, I doubled down and shook my head.

"You tell me why you trust Blackstone and I might share what I know." So weird to be on the other side of my dad. It had happened before, I'd doubted him in the past. Even thought him capable of murder. But I would never in a million years have believed he'd side with a corporation against his own town's best interest.

"This isn't a game, young lady," Dad snapped, standing up abruptly, hands falling to his sides. I'd never seen him so angry.

"No, it's not." I wasn't getting anywhere, clearly. "This is bigger than Reading, Dad. Bigger than murder."

He didn't flinch. "Have you told Crew?" Wow, that sounded bitter.

"As a matter of fact, I haven't," I snapped back. "I made a promise to a source." My jaw tightened despite my internal command to relax, slow down, let it go. This was my father I was holding out against. Not my enemy.

He closed the distance between us, looming over me. Not threatening—he was my dad. But definitely laying on the pressure. I'd seen him do this to suspects before, using his height and his bulk to his advantage. Thing was, I was his daughter, not some perp. Intimidation didn't work on me.

"Fee," he said, growling voice deep and low.

"Dad," I said, an impulsive question leaping into my mind as, in a flash of inspiration, a white card with a name drawn in block letters appeared in an instant of memory. "Who is Siobhan Doyle?"

Back in October, when I'd attended the séance at Sadie Hatch's place, I'd been exposed to her fake ghosts and apparitions, her attempt to prove she was psychic giving me the shivers. The renderings of the dead she'd offered up had been holographic, technology developed by her grandson, Denver. While I knew they were fake, there had been one, the ghost of Manuel Cortez, that still gave me shivery goosebumps when I thought about him, if only because both Denver and his girlfriend, Alice, claimed that particular apparition might have been real.

Whatever. Still, the memory scared me to this day, and I tried not to think about it. Except in the moment I mentioned the woman's name from the card Malcolm Murray handed me, the fear of seeing that dead young man's spirit came rushing back. Not because he appeared to me, not at all. No, it was the way Dad's face lost all color, turning ashen and pale as if he were the one who saw a ghost at the mere mention of her.

He gaped at me a long moment, cold sweat breaking out on his upper lip, eyes wide and staring. I reached out to touch his hand, terrified by what I witnessed, only to have him shake himself almost like a dog shedding water before backing away abruptly, one big hand rising to swipe over his open mouth.

Dad spun and stormed out of the kitchen, striding so fast on his long legs for the exit and with such abrupt speed by the time I got moving to follow him he was already out the front door, not quite slamming it shut behind him. And while I watched him go with my heart in my throat, I made myself a promise in the quiet of the foyer of Petunia's with my pug whining softly at my feet.

As soon as the wedding was over and this whole murder case was behind me, I had a phone call to make. Devastating or not, I had to know what secret Siobhan Doyle held and why it terrified my father.

CHAPTER TWENTY-NINE

Mom breezed her way around the kitchen of the annex, humming softly to herself while I scowled into my coffee and thought about blurting out a question that haunted me since Malcolm handed me a business card in the back of his town car. The same question I asked Dad the night before. But I couldn't bring myself to ruin her mood, not after she'd been in such a state the last few months only to reemerge as my long-lost mother thanks to a mysterious person I needed to hug as hard as I could for helping her recover her sense of self.

Instead, I grumped into my mug and let her enjoy her morning and the sunshine pouring into the modern, stainless-steel kitchen. While I'd insisted on maintaining some charm in the remainder of the remodel, this space I'd given over to convection ovens and polished counters and a durable cork flooring meant to go easy on the feet of those who worked here. Mom seemed delighted by the choices Jared and I made, her sneakers squeaking faintly while she examined every nook and cranny with her prim blue apron snug around her waist.

I left her for the foyer at the sound of the front door chime, wondering if Pamela and Fleur had come to get me or if I was going to make the lonely walk to Crew's office alone. I'd meant to go at 9AM, to get it over with like tearing off a particularly uncomfortable bandage the moment Daisy and the staff had breakfast in hand. But Mom's insistence I join her at the annex while she looked around was the excuse I needed to hide out and not spill what I'd learned to the overtaxed and likely snarky sheriff.

Instead of the two journalists, I found myself saluting Jared and Aiden with my rapidly cooling coffee, the sight of the friends not really alleviating my mood as much as solidifying it. Didn't help that Jared looked faintly embarrassed, likely thanks to his fistfight of the day before, or that Aiden's pinched and worried expression woke the memory of his girlfriend's infidelity.

Amazing start to the day. Couldn't wait to see what happened from here.

"Have you seen Carmen?" Speaking of said girlfriend. Aiden had his hands in his back pockets, Jared's face darkening a little.

I stammered a denial, though it was impossible for him to know about what I'd seen the night before, right? I had zero reason to stutter nervously the negative while Jared's scowl deepened. I now suspected the reason my friend had gotten into the altercation with Philip—had he witnessed what I witnessed if at a different time?—and wondered if he guessed why I was acting oddly.

Grace's door opened and she joined me in the foyer, refusing to look at either Jared or Aiden, her round face rested though her eyes appeared a bit bloodshot from crying. "Are you serving breakfast?"

I turned to gesture at the kitchen, to tell her to trot herself to Petunia's before Daisy wrapped the last of the morning's offerings when Philip's door at the top of the stairs opened and he emerged. But he wasn't alone, was he? Oh, no. No, he was not. Just my freaking luck to be witness to the attractive young brunette who exited behind him.

Carmen had to choose right then to break Aiden's heart?

Oh, crap.

I wasn't the only one to take in her rumpled t-shirt, her damp hair fresh from the shower, the guilty and horrified look on her face when she stopped abruptly about halfway down the stairs with her dark eyes locked on Aiden's stricken face. I wanted to rush to him and turn him around, push him outside so he didn't have to witness her betrayal so blatantly. And to avoid the inevitable meltdown I felt to the core of my being, the far too familiar blow to the gut that was the moment of reveal the person you loved had stabbed you in the heart.

I remembered staring in shock at Ryan and the girl he'd fumbled around under the sheets of our bed. I recalled clearly and with great agony the moment he stood with his face red, and his hips covered with the corner of the comforter I'd bought for us just a week prior, the feather-filled softness of it taking up the bulk of my tips for the month. I lived in that moment as Aiden inhaled, his face contorting from surprised hurt to utter rage and couldn't shake free even when he lunged, shouting incoherently, toward the staircase and the stunned and silent Philip.

Thankfully, Jared was thinking straight, if the only one in the foyer to do so. He caught his friend by the arm and wrestled him into an awkward-looking headlock. It didn't stop Aiden from continuing his audible barrage of swearing and calling Carmen some rather unpleasant things. She pushed past Philip, her own voice adding to the cacophony I barely registered, honestly, my mental connection to the moment of my own hurt so powerful I staggered from it.

And snapped back into reality, suddenly and with the kind of clarity that stung, before lunging for the three young people now tussling in my entry, my own voice booming over their shouts.

"OUTSIDE!"

Jared flinched, Carmen pulling back from her attempt to hit Aiden while he continued to shout at her.

"I'm not kidding!" I jabbed a finger at them. "Not in my annex! You three want to act like children, good on you. But do it on the freaking sidewalk!"

Jared physically dragged Aiden out of the foyer and down the steps, Carmen following after them, while I panted through my reaction to the scene. I spun to find Grace had slunk off, Philip with her, and good riddance. The sound of shouting intensified from the street, but I didn't care, not even when the wail of a siren broke through the screaming of profanities, Crew's deep, angry voice booming over the shrieking Carmen defiantly threw back at him.

Mom came running, her eyes huge, her hands on her heart, pausing next to me while I gripped my mug so tightly, I was sure I'd crush the ceramic if I wasn't careful. She met my eyes while I caught my breath, hugging me a moment.

"What happened?"

"Doesn't matter," I said through gritted teeth. The sound of fighting diminished, Crew's voice dropping from a shout to a more reasonable volume, though still audible through the open door.

I forced myself to exit the foyer, to descend the steps and join the gathering, though I winced at the few guests of mine who gathered outside Petunia's, witnesses to the meltdown unfolding so publicly.

Aiden openly wept while Carmen scowled at Crew who was talking to her with his head down, his hand on her arm. The sheriff glanced up and met my eyes a moment, his gaze steady but cold and I felt myself contract as I remembered I had more than

Fleur's information to talk to him about. Robert's grin wasn't helping any, nor was his repeated hand gesture from the night before as he aimed his index finger at me and pulled the trigger.

Crew straightened from talking to Carmen, turning toward Aiden who no longer fought Jared, sniffling as he wiped at his face with the collar of his now stretched-out *Zip It!* t-shirt.

"The next person who gets into a fistfight on my streets gets charged with assault." He sounded angry but controlled, gruffly confident. Aiden nodded, stared at his feet, while Jared held up both hands in defeat. Only Carmen seemed defiant, tossing her dark hair. Crew looked up at me again, tipped his hat. But there was little warmth in the gesture, a stiffness that made me sigh.

"Ms. Flemings," he said.

Right, Mom was with me. "Sheriff," I said. "I need to talk to you."

Wouldn't you know, Matt chose that exact moment to pull up to the front of the annex and climb out, his eyes locked on me? The instant he appeared Crew's face shut down and I knew in that heartbeat not only had Robert run to the sheriff with his ridiculous story, the handsome man I thought I was getting to know believed him. At least, enough to trigger doubt that crossed his face as clearly as if he'd said so out loud.

Now, maybe if things had been different, I would have reacted better. Possibly without the kind of temperamental fireworks that exploded in my chest as if he'd accused me of cheating when we weren't even really going out—technicalities be damned. But the trouble was, I'd just been through a highly emotional slam dunk down a memory superhighway that dragged me behind the worst day of my life. So, forgive me if I kind of lost my cool for a second and shot Crew the kind of deathly stare that could easily have ended in the sort of altercation he'd just put an end to.

I loved my mother. She might not have had any idea what was actually going on, but she had the best instincts on the planet when it came to me, and that morning was no exception. With a kindly but firm hand on my arm, she tugged me against her side and pinched me firmly with the other, so hard I twitched and met her gaze rather than hurtling myself at Robert in an attempt to gouge his eyes out.

"Crew." Matt seemed oblivious to everything going on around him, Carmen and Aiden not the least of the mess. To his credit, he seemed pretty upset, though he could take a freaking number.

The sheriff turned slowly toward him as if debating what he was going to do next. Wow, was he really buying into what Robert said that much? Seriously. All the anger ran out of me, replaced suddenly by cold hurt. Okay, so I was a bit of a roller coaster, no judging. No one had the right to do that to me.

Meanwhile, I was judging Carmen, wasn't I?

"I need to talk to you." Matt's agitation cut through everything. Crew finally faced him, and even

I paid attention.

"I'll be right with you." Crew turned back, sighed, shoulders sagging just a fraction. "Do I need to cart the three of you off to jail for the day or are we on the same page?"

"We're good, Sheriff," Jared said. "Come on, Aiden."

Carmen shrugged, looking miserable now that she'd had time to diffuse her own temper. "Aiden…"

He staggered away from her, Jared's arm around his shoulders. She slunk off down the street on her own, arms around herself, though where she was going, I had no idea. And didn't care. Not when Matt, bouncing on the balls of his feet, caught Crew's attention again.

Crew nodded to him, clearly cranky but listening. "What happened?"

"Someone broke into the station last night." Matt's eyes met mine for a moment and he nodded to me. I sighed when Crew's eyes followed his gaze, wanting to shout at the sheriff for what I assumed he was thinking despite having no idea what was actually going through his mind. Damn it. "Whoever it was stole some evidence I found."

Crew's head came up, scowl replacing the faint frown he'd worn a moment ago. "What evidence?"

Matt flushed, looking at me again. "I meant to share, but I wanted to find out more first."

I guess I earned the glare the sheriff shot at me. "See what you started?" Wait, what? "Everyone's a damned detective now." I hardly needed to mention

Matt was a freaking park ranger with a gun and a badge and investigative training, did I?

From the hangdog look Matt gave me I suspected, however, Crew was not only right but the ranger held back the evidence in some kind of misguided attempt at impressing me. I would have smacked him if I was closer. Instead, I fumed where I stood while Crew's jaw jumped, tic starting up like clockwork.

"What did you find?" His deep voice rumbled gravel.

"A lens cap," Matt said, "a big one, like off one of those giant telephoto attachments." Now where had I seen one of those recently? Damn it, Fleur.

"Where?" Crew sounded interested at last.

"In the tree," Matt said, faint misery in his voice. "Where Lewis was found." He tossed his hands as he finished like he knew he'd screwed up and didn't know how to make things right. "There was blood on it."

CHAPTER THIRTY

Crew didn't get to chastise him, because my blurtiness interceded.

"The body was bloodless," I said. I knew intimately because I'd hung on the line with it (him) for quite some time. "So, whose blood was it?"

"We need to ask that of Fleur King," Matt said. "The owner's name was etched on the cap."

And that told me I already guessed who it belonged to. Awesome.

Mom tugged at me as I left the step to go to Matt while Crew answered his ringing phone, turning his back on me to talk quietly into it. I soothed my mother's anxiety with a pat to her hand, so she'd know I wasn't about to murder Robert in full view of everyone after all before stopping at Matt's side with my hands clenched into fists.

Okay, so maybe I wouldn't be killing my cousin, but the misguided ranger in front of me? Oooh. Boys.

"What the hell were you thinking withholding evidence?" Because I wasn't a snooping busybody who'd held a few things back from Crew in the past. Uh-huh.

Matt flinched, running one hand through his hair, before grinning weakly at me. "I'm sorry. I was going to show it to you last night and we were interrupted."

Oh, no, he did *not* just put this mess on me. "Nice try," I snapped, keeping my voice down. "You should know better."

He blushed again. "I do," he said. "It's just... Fee." He cleared his throat, looked around and I realized he was about to start saying things that really shouldn't be said on a sidewalk out in public with the man I wanted to date turning slowly toward us, still talking on the phone. Ack. "I was a jackass last night. I know you and Crew..." he hesitated again, and I almost whacked him to stop him from stuttering out what he said next. Instead, I held my breath and did my best not to wince. "I've been trying to work up the courage to ask you out since you got home."

Well, hell in a handbasket. He had to tell me now?

"Nice going," I shot back. "What, I was supposed to guess or something?" Sheesh.

He laughed, clearly uncomfortable. "Yeah?"

Okay, that got a grin out of me, an easing of my temper from the sheer idiocy of the moment.

"You're not just a jackass," I said. "You're blind." I shook my head at him, sighed out the last of the tension I'd carried since I agreed to keep my mouth shut last night in Pamela's office and decided regardless of what he now thought of me, Crew would be getting an earful from Fiona Fleming, like it or not. For now, though, I had some advice to deliver, Matt frowning at my last statement. "If you're into blondes, I know one in particular who'd be delighted if you'd get off your hands and ask her out."

Matt's face lit up and he glanced at Petunia's so fast I felt a bit hurt at the shift in his attention. "Daisy?"

I was going to punch him for real. "Just ask Jill out, would you? You're killing me here."

This time he looked like I *had* hit him before his shock turned to speculation. I walked away from him while the wheels turned—wishing her luck because apparently, he wasn't as swift as I'd thought, at least when it came to women—and joined Crew as he hung up on his caller.

"No sign of the owner of the lens cap," he said like he expected I'd be asking. "She's one of the media, a photojournalist."

"Yes," I said, "and I have a lot to tell you about her. I take it she and Pamela didn't show up at your office this morning." Well, too bad. She had her night to sort things out. I was done protecting her story.

Crew shook his head, blue eyes intent. "Leave it

to you to have what I need."

I wasn't sure how to take that but chose to brush off any negative implications. "If you're interested in talking to her," I said, turning my back on him, "I'll be at Petunia's. Knocking on her door."

He followed me without a word, waving to Mom on the way by. She watched me with careful eyes, but I ignored her and kept moving, head high, nodding to the guests exiting the front door of my B&B while I did my best to show Crew Turner I couldn't care less if he judged me or not.

A quick check of Fleur's room turned up an empty space, the photojournalist long gone. Crew stood in the middle of the abandoned suite with his hands on his hips, head down, eyes shadowed by his hat. He looked rather delicious in the dim light with a patch of sun beaming down at the tips of his boots, dust motes floating past the tan of his uniform shirt pulled taunt across his broad shoulders, his most shapely posterior firmly contained inside his blue jeans. I wanted to push back the dark hair curving over his collar, knowing from experience how soft his waves were. To cup that strong, tight jaw in my hands, run my thumbs over the faint stubble and feel the warmth of his lips on my mouth.

Growl. For the last time, down, girl.

Instead, I planted myself in his way so he couldn't run for the hills and spoke into the quiet of the room, telling him everything I'd learned from the moment we'd parted until the fight on the street outside just a few minutes ago, leaving out nothing.

Including my encounter with Matt.

Crew didn't respond, listening and holding still, while I used a crisp and calculated tone to share everything I knew. I did my best to stay impartial, to drop all of my information in the exacting and logical way I knew got through to him the most clearly. But when I finished and he didn't move, I snapped, my temper waking once more despite myself.

"Now you know what I know," I said. "Except this final thing, Crew Turner." That turned his head, caught his attention, his blue eyes fixing on me, silent and watchful. "If you plan to listen to someone like Robert Carlisle over trusting me, if you want to be a jealous ass who judges something he didn't even witness, you can take a walk right now and keep walking." I stepped aside from the door to the room and gestured for him to go. "Because I'm not that girl. And I never will be."

Now, in all honesty, I had no idea what he was thinking, or even if my worry about what he might have surmised from Robert's little tattle tale session was a reality or fantasy. I was running on instinct, obviously, and the renewal of the hurt I'd felt when Ryan cheated on me and left me bereft and adrift. So, to be fair, this wasn't about Crew, and I likely sounded far more over-reactive than I needed to be. But there it was and there we were.

Crew exhaled into the quiet dimness, hands dropping from his hips. He closed the distance between us in two strides. I had no idea the misery that engulfed my heart until he embraced me, hugging me tightly to his broad chest. In that moment the hurt lifted, and I suppressed a shudder at its passing.

"I know," he whispered. "Robert's a jerk. And so am I."

So, he *had* doubted. I couldn't bring myself to be angry anymore. Well, not much.

"I have no idea what's wrong with me." Crew pushed me back, smiled down at me, open honesty in his gaze, the man I was falling in love with standing before me again. "You've been patient and I'm being ridiculous." He bent and pressed his lips to my forehead, the brim of his hat brushing over my hair. "God, you make me crazy. You know that?"

I choked on my answer before finding my voice again. "Same here."

We stood a long moment, absorbed in each other, while my heartbeat returned to normal and the fear and doubt and judgment I'd turned against myself—Ryan had so much to answer for and I had a lot of digging out of what was left of him to do—withered and died under Crew's calm, gentle gaze.

I kissed him finally, just a short, sweet touch of his lips on mine before punching his arm. He grinned, rubbing the spot like it hurt (poor baby) and sighed.

"No kissing on the job," he said, gruff but teasing.

"Whatever," I eye-rolled.

He stepped around me, his turn to gesture at the door. "Miss Fleming."

"Where are we going?" I arched an eyebrow at him but preceded him out into the hall without an answer.

"I have a photojournalist to chat with," he said, paused to smile at me. "I could use an introduction." Another brief moment of quiet followed. "Are you coming or not?"

CHAPTER THIRTY-ONE

Of course, when we arrived at the *Gazette* office, the doors were locked and despite a call to the house, Aundrea informed us the journalists weren't home.

"Pamela's not answering her phone." Aundrea sounded nervous, but that was a typical state for her, so I did my best to reassure her before signing off.

Crew frowned at his hands where they rested on the steering wheel, eyes distant. "Would Fleur King have a motive to kill Lewis Brown?"

Hmmm. There was an idea I hadn't considered. "She seemed pretty adamant about keeping her story to herself until she published it," I said. "But wouldn't she want him alive when she did that?"

Crew nodded. "I was thinking the same thing. It's not like hanging him from the zip line was a crime of anger, either. So, if he confronted her about her story, wouldn't she just have maybe struck him in defense?"

"Exactly," I said, staring out the window at the passing foot traffic, at the towering statue of Captain Reading and sighed, headshaking over the graffiti phallic symbol the local unknown artist refreshed sometime last night on the front of the bronze's breeches. "Why make a statement like that? Take the time to hang him before sending him down the zip line?"

"How about Philip Davis?" Crew turned to meet my eyes, leaning one big shoulder against the side window as he pivoted toward me, voice deep and thoughtful. "If Blackstone is behind the fake woodpecker story, would they want to stir up controversy by killing off their bought and paid-for protestor? I would think their typical process would be a quiet ending and murder doesn't play into that."

"Unless Philip took matters into his own hands." Did I believe that? He'd sounded annoyed on the phone, angry about the circumstances. "Who does that leave?"

"Aiden and Carmen," Crew said. Hesitated. "Jared."

"Again, why go to all the trouble of setting up the park to take the fall?" I sighed as I chewed my bottom lip. "It's their livelihood, right? Their dream." Carmen's at least. "What if Aiden knew about Carmen and Philip and was trying to ruin her?" But didn't he have his own stake in *Zip It!*? "Do you know if they were all equal partners?"

"Actually, most of the money came from Carmen," Crew said, nodding as he followed my train of thought. "And Jared. She inherited from her parents when they died and invested that trust fund in the park. Aiden had a small nest egg and Jared fronted the rest. But the majority of the risk was hers."

"So, if Aiden wanted to hurt her for hurting him…" Still, murder was a long way to go. "I could see him killing Philip, maybe. But why Lewis Brown?" It didn't make any sense. "And if Lewis was working for Blackstone, could it have been some other protestor?" I thought about Grace. "What about his partner?"

Crew shook his head. "I'm afraid Fleur is off base there," he said. "I know for a fact Lewis wasn't working for Blackstone."

Oh really. "Former FBI coworkers come through for you, maybe?" I didn't mean to approach that information so archly, but Crew flinched a bit before shrugging.

"I meant to tell you," he said. "Didn't seem important for you to know I used to be with the Bureau."

Uh-huh. "Why would she think so, then?"

"He was recently under investigation," Crew said, "for his part in the fraudulent claims of endangered species popping up around the country. Turns out he was getting paid quite well to chase the claims. But there's no connection to Blackstone."

"Then who was paying him?" That didn't make

sense either.

"Some shell corporation," Crew said. "The FBI is still chasing down who owns it, but they suspect from the online payment activity it's an activist fund, privately owned and meant for jobs such as this, to sabotage land sales to large companies. Trouble is, if they're breaking the law, while it might be well-intentioned it's still illegal."

I didn't comment that sometimes illegal action against corporations like Blackstone might be the only defense for small towns like ours. "If Lewis wasn't working for Blackstone, we're back to Philip. He might have killed him and set up the murder to make an example of Lewis and the people funding him." Something still didn't feel right.

"We both saw him just prior," Crew said, staring out the windshield now.

"It wouldn't have taken much to get his hands on some of the line that was used to strangle Lewis," I said.

Crew grunted. "Aiden confirmed the rope used was the same that was taken from *Zip It!* that morning."

"The theft happened pretty early on, though it was Aiden who specifically reported it." To hide his tracks? "Philip is a pretty solid guy. If Lewis was already up the tree…" I left it hanging. No pun intended. "What about the footprint? The discarded sign at the bottom of the tree?" I thought about Matt, wondered if he'd forwarded the image to Crew or not.

"Jill spotted it," he said. "It's on my list. I have her checking shoes, but there were a ton of people there that day. Not only have most of them already skipped town, the few we managed to take imprints from all wore the same brand so it's a bit of a dead end." He sounded about as frustrated as I felt.

"I still maintain the lens cap isn't a clue," I said. "There was no blood on Lewis's body."

"Agreed," Crew said. "It's likely Fleur climbed the tree to take pictures of the crime scene and left it behind. Still, I want to ask her that directly."

"Did Dr. Aberstock confirm strangulation as the cause of death?" I picked at a stray thread on the thigh of my jeans as my mind turned over and over.

"He did," Crew said. "No other signs of trauma." He reached over and squeezed my hand. "The fact is, Carmen has an alibi, despite chasing Philip. Lewis died in the window she was with the reporters. But Philip didn't appear on camera, and she chased him after Lewis was dead." Okay then. "Aiden is off the hook, too, from the footage I viewed. But Jared isn't, Fee." Well, that sucked. "I'm going to have to bring him in for questioning."

Maybe I should have been more worried. Except I had little doubt my friend was innocent, so I shrugged. "Alicia was there."

"Not until after you found the body." He was being careful with me. I really needed to cut him some slack if he felt he couldn't be honest.

"You have a job to do, Crew," I said. "So do it. But if you think Jared has a motive, I'd like to hear it."

Crew sighed softly, squeezing my fingers. "If I've learned one thing on this job, it's that people's motivations are about as convoluted as the idiotic politics in this town." I couldn't argue with him there. "Let's think about it, though. If Jared thought Lewis was working for Blackstone, maybe he saw him as a threat. Everyone knows the kid's been overworked since his father died and left him holding a bag of fraudulent business dealings as deep as Cutter Lake." He didn't have to remind me. "Lewis was threatening his venture, his friends. He might have snapped." I wasn't so sure about that. Crew must have sensed my argument because he went on in that same level, logical tone. "I have enough evidence of his failing temper, Fee," he said. "If two fights in public aren't enough for you, I don't know what is."

I almost spoke up, offered excuses, and realized he was right. The Jared I knew was on the edge. I'd seen it in him before this even started. And hadn't Carmen mentioned she was worried about him? But did that make him capable of murder? "I'm going to back away from that," I said, hating that my tone was so soft and unsure. This was Jared we were talking about. "He was defending his friend."

"And his business." Crew sounded bummed about it, at least. "I like him too, Fee, but."

But.

"I have it on good authority that Jared has stretched himself pretty thin these days. Financially, emotionally, mentally. He's trying too hard, Fee, and that's a dangerous combination."

Damn him, why did Crew have to be right? Just enough I doubted?

Crew seemed like he didn't want to go on before he released my hand and spoke again, this time without looking at me. On purpose. "I'll have to talk to your father, too."

That made two of us. "Dad had no motive for murder." But he was working for Blackstone and Philip Davis. That still rankled, honestly.

Crew laughed at that, a rumbling sound without an edge that woke a grin on my own face. "Don't worry," he chuckled, rubbing his eyes with his thumb and index finger before sighing out the last of his amusement. "I'm not even going there. The Fleming family gets a pass from now on unless I catch one of you in the act or with the murder weapon." He winked at me, blue eyes sparkling. "Anyone else?"

"Just Lewis's fellow activists," I said. "If they thought he betrayed them...? Sold them out?" They were a pretty passionate bunch. "Grace?"

Crew thought about it a moment. "A definite possibility," he said. "But she's older and not very agile, from what I've seen. According to the footage, she didn't take a harness or helmet. She left the climbing to Lewis." I would have to trust him on that, I guess, since asking to see said footage would likely end in a resounding no. "Could she have even made it up the tree?"

"She might have had help." I thought about her

reaction to his death. "She seemed really broken up by his loss." A good actress or innocent of wrongdoing? I clenched my hands in my lap as the last pool of suspects crossed my mind. "What about the Pattersons?"

Crew didn't respond right away. When he finally answered, he sounded thoughtful, not worried, despite his words. "I don't want to think about them right now."

Hmmm. Okay then.

Crew drove me home, pulling up in front of Petunia's. Before I could leave the cab, he put the truck in park and leaned toward me, one hand sliding around my neck, cradling my head as he bent close and kissed me. My heart rate quickly increased, my breath catching as his lips parted from mine after a long, lovely moment.

"Keep me posted, Master Detective," he said. Grinned.

I grinned back. "You too, G-Man," I winked.

Crew laughed and let me go. "Get out of my truck," he growled.

I watched him drive away from the curb, wondering how many more secrets of his I'd have to uncover and shivering a bit at the delight of knowing I'd get the chance.

CHAPTER THIRTY-TWO

I wasn't expecting to have to field a phone call the minute I stepped through the door to Petunia's, but Daisy was busy with a pair of guests and from her slightly frantic expressions she'd been dealing with the aftermath of the fight outside the annex since I left with Crew.

Whoops. I quickly picked up the receiver and used my best chipper tone. "Thanks for calling Petunia's Bed and Breakfast, Fiona speaking, can I help you?"

The voice on the other end sounded about as upset as any I'd ever heard. "Fee," Margaret said, "I have terrible news." It took me a moment to recognize her voice, to identify her as Vivian's manager and shift gears from murder to wedding plans, but as I piece together who it was, she rushed on. "I'm so sorry to tell you this, I don't know how it happened." She sounded near to tears, her normally calm and confident tone utterly frazzled. "We're totally overbooked, and the cake meant for the wedding has disappeared. I think it was used for someone else's event."

Um, okay, no panic on my end. "So, make another one...?" Right? Logic dictated, didn't it?

"You don't understand," Margaret wailed. "I can't fit in another project. I'm on my way out of state for a last-minute political event and every one of my bakers is totally booked. Fee, I'm sorry, we have to cancel."

She had to... I choked on the words coming across the line at me while my heart skipped a painful beat. "You can't do this to me," I hissed into the receiver. "The wedding is Saturday." It was freaking Thursday. Was she kidding me?

"I know, I know, I'm sorry." She sounded like she was crying. "I'm totally overextended, and everything is a disaster. I've had two bakers quit on me the last three days, had six events added to my calendar and now this." Margaret exhaled like she was ready to crack. "Fee, I'm so sorry, but something has to give. And you're it." Without another word, she hung up on me, leaving me staring at the phone in my hand while everything closed in around me and I swear, if I hadn't leaned against the wall beside me, I would have passed out.

No. Not so close to the wedding day. I had days left, not weeks. What was I going to—

I hung up and raced for the kitchen, the back door, hoofing it across the yard to the annex and my salvation. She stood in the stainless-steel perfection of the new house, auburn hair perfectly styled, green eyes glowing with delight as she puttered around like she'd been born to cook, making lunch and smiling at me.

"Mom," I gasped. "The cake!"

Her gaze widencd, lips parting slightly as I filled her in. And then, with a graciousness that soothed my panicked heart, she bobbed her head with a tiny smile. An expression that woke a horrible notion inside me.

"Of course, I can handle it, sweetie," she said, waving me off with a wooden spoon. "Just leave it to your mother."

Sneaking suspicions aside, I have to admit I felt better save for the rush of adrenaline that I now combatted, hoping it would wear off before it gave me a heart attack or a headache. A stroke. An aneurysm. Something deadly.

Argh.

As I crossed back to Petunia's and left Mom to her new assignment—her old one, to be honest—I couldn't help but feel sick over who it was I now suspected gave Mom her mojo back. She was far too gracious about this whole disaster, not the least bit surprised, actually. Which meant, to my investigative brain, she had an inkling of what was coming.

And that meant someone warned her ahead of time.

No. I couldn't be grateful. Wouldn't. Except, of course, I had my mother back. Thanks to the one person on the planet I detested more than my cousin Robert.

Not thinking about this right now, thanks. Not.

I almost ran into Grace in the garden, grateful for the distraction and practically latching onto her on my way by just to shake off the thoughts trying to win me over. The activist seemed startled and more than a little off-put by my desperate self, but she didn't run away when I pulled her down on a bench and gasped out a question.

"Did you know about Lewis's connection to the Blackstone Corporation?" Okay, so Crew said he wasn't connected, but I wanted to hear that from the horse's mouth.

Grace looked instantly offended, her nose scrunching in response, eyes flat and cold. "He had no such ties," she said. "My Lewis would never betray the cause like that."

"So, who was paying him?" Wow, Fee, way to be all confrontational and demanding. Apparently, that was the best way to tackle Grace, however, because she sat up a little straighter, replying with the kind of prim focus meant to shut down opposition.

"I have no idea what you're talking about," she said. "Lewis only ever protested for altruistic purposes. He would never have accepted payment. How abhorrent."

"Not even if that money was raised by other activists?" I shook my head, knowing what she was going to say before she said it. "You do know he was under investigation by the FBI for fabricating endangered species sightings?"

That made her flinch. "I am aware," she said.

"Any truth to it?" Bluntness as a weapon of choice? I was clearly in a terrible state of mind.

Again, though, it seemed to do the trick. "I can assure you," she said, "Lewis had no idea whatsoever of any kind of falsehood. He acted only in the best interests of the flora and fauna he sought to protect." She fanned herself, eyes moist. "Honestly, your questions leave me breathless." She stood abruptly. "If you'll excuse me." Grace hurried off and I almost went after her. The only problem with that plan? As I lurched to my feet to follow, a dark-haired young woman, sobbing as she ran, hurtled herself at me and hugged me so hard she knocked me off balance and back onto the bench.

Carmen clung to me a moment before leaning away, tears pouring down her cheeks, her thick, black hair clinging to the moisture.

"Have you seen him?" I shook my head at her, not sure who she was referring to. "Philip?" Ah, him.

"No, sorry." Not sorry.

Carmen burst into tears again, hands over her face. "I know what you think of me," she choked. "I hate myself, Fee. But him more." She looked up with pure rage in her eyes. "When I find him, I'm going to strangle him." Oh, really? She flinched like she knew what she said didn't sound very good, considering how Lewis Brown died on her property. Did she and

Aiden have something to do with his death after all? "After Aiden left, Philip told me he only slept with me to ruin our relationship." She sagged against the bench, looking defeated and crumpled, face aged past her early twenties. "To ruin our business so Blackstone could buy the land out from under us at a cut-rate price." Interesting and confirmation of part of Fleur's story. How had she gotten Lewis's involvement and payoff wrong, then?

"Carmen, no offense," I said, not caring if she took any, "but you must have suspected something when he just showed up in your life again like that. Knowing who he worked for."

She fluttered her hands at me. "I knew what he did for a living," she said. "But I was blind. Aiden is everything to me, but Philip was my first love." Carmen took a shaking breath, seemed to settle somewhat. "I couldn't believe he'd do that to me."

"I can." I half turned to find Aiden standing behind us, head down, face as ashen as Carmen's. She meeped out a little sigh of distress at the sight of him. "Thing is, as much as I hate to give him what he wants, Philip's getting his wish." He refused to meet her eyes. "I'm selling out my portion of *Zip It!* to Blackstone, Carmen. I'm done."

She leaped to her feet, tried to lunge for him, but I caught her and held her back. But she didn't try to hurt him. Her face twisted in grief as she fell against me. "Please," she whispered. "Our dream."

Did he realize she seemed to value it more than him? Apparently. "This isn't my dream," Aiden said, backing away with his grief written all over his young face. "Yours, Carmen." He laughed softly, full of pain. "I would have followed you anywhere, supported anything you wanted." He tossed his hands, finally met her eyes, anger flashing, stiffening his back, bringing his head up. "Your loss. I'm done. Screw you and your damned park. Good luck running it with Blackstone breathing down your neck." He half-turned before stopping. "Oh, and Jared's out, too. So, I think that gives them enough control to make your life the misery you've made mine."

Aiden left without another word spoken, Carmen collapsing in my arms while I did my best to fight the urge to just drop her on her ass.

CHAPTER THIRTY-THREE

One benefit to Fleur vanishing and Philip taking a hike? I quickly moved Grace into the room vacated by the photojournalist and handed over the keys of the annex to the decorators who moved on the place like their lives depended on it and just in time.

I did one last sweep of the vacated rooms, surprised to find Fleur King's card on the floor under Philip's dresser. What was he doing with it? I really needed to track her down, not to mention the now absent Blackstone liaison. He'd vanished from town without a trace, from what I could tell. And so far any attempt to find Fleur or Pamela for that matter met with nothing. I was beginning to wonder if Aundrea's worries about her missing fiancé were valid, except of course the constant phone calls I fielded the rest of the morning to that effect made me stop caring if Pamela was dead at the bottom of a ditch or on her way to the Caribbean with who I now suspected was an old flame.

Shame on you, Fee. Have a bit of compassion.

With lunch over, I abandoned Daisy to handle things—bless her for never once complaining—and headed out to check the *Gazette* for the missing journalists. The front door, now open, allowed me entry to the newsroom, though it took a bit of hunting to track down the two women.

It was a good thing I noticed the red light on over the door, or I would have barged right into the darkroom instead of knocking heavily. After a brief hissing discussion, the light turned green and the door swung inward, Pamela latching onto me and dragging me inside before the illumination overhead switched to crimson.

Fleur didn't seem all that happy to see me, but Pamela was grinning like a wild woman, so I chose to act like I was welcome by all parties and peered around the taller woman at the images she was developing.

"Who prints anything anymore?" I hadn't meant to ask that out loud while Fleur sighed heavily as if I'd insulted her entire way of life. Well, maybe I had.

"Technocrat," Fleur muttered, softly swirling a sheet of photo paper in some kind of fluid. The lines over the table she used were cluttered with images of Lewis, Grace, Philip, the park. Carmen and the aforementioned in a passionate embrace. Aiden and Jared. Even me, grinning as I zipped. I prodded

Pamela when I leaned away, the same moment she glanced at her vibrating phone.

"If you don't let your fiancé know you're still alive so she stops calling me every five seconds I'm seriously going to dump your body in the woods where no one will find you."

She winked at me, though the faint frown on Fleur's face told me volumes. "I'll call her in a bit," she said.

"I'm worried about Jared." I rubbed my upper arms with both hands, the chill in the room making goosebumps rise on my skin. Too much air conditioning. "Crew seems to think he's pushing himself too far."

Pamela's instant scoff and eye roll was about as encouraging as I was going to get. "Please. That kid's more stable than we are. He's fine. Besides, he has the family behind him, no matter what they think of me and his mother." Good to know. Though it did raise the question of the Pattersons and their involvement in all this. "Besides, he was with me when Lewis was killed." Phew. I needed to tell Crew. Her lips twisted a moment, a bit of guilt flashing on her face. "He probably didn't tell the sheriff because he did me a solid, sneaking me in before Carmen and Aiden invited the rest of the group inside. Hung out with me until we heard you screaming. Then he ran to your rescue." All of that sounded like Jared.

"What about Fleur? Did he let her in, too?" I raised an eyebrow at the tall journalist.

Pamela paused long enough I figured out what

she was going to say before she said it. "Jared doesn't know about Fleur." There were whole volumes of unspoken words in that simple statement.

Which meant Aundrea didn't know about Fleur either.

"Please," the slim photographer said as she swished her photo. "I've covered stories around the world in war-torn countries and gang-controlled corners of urban centers. I think I can sneak into a zip line park without being spotted."

I was just relieved Jared had an alibi. "So, does that mean you're not a stranger to death, Fleur?"

She turned her head to grin at me, angular face sharply in focus and rather sinister in the red lighting. "Are you asking me if I killed Lewis Brown?"

"Just answer her, Fleur," Pamela sighed.

Before she could, I flipped out her card and showed it to her. "Found this in the room Philip rented from me," I said. "In the annex. Where you shouldn't have had the chance to set foot. So tell me, Ms. King, while you're giving me your answer about the murder—why were you talking with the Blackstone infiltrator?" Her gaze dropped to the card, met my eyes again. "And why, oh why your bloody lens cap from your telephoto attachment was found in the tree where the body was discovered only to be stolen from the custody of the park ranger who discovered it?"

Pamela's eyebrows arched as she crossed her arms over her chest, tapping her fingertips on her forearm. "You've been a busy little flower," she said.

Fleur tsked at her, clearly irritated now. "I tried to talk to Philip Davis about his involvement with Blackstone," she grunted that answer. "I threatened to tell the protestors who he was and he got rough with me. I had to fight him off. So, the blood you'll find on the cap? It's his." I'd assumed the damage to Philip's nose had been all Jared from the punch he delivered, but if Fleur got to him first? "As for the cap itself, I needed it back." She grinned suddenly. "That ranger? He left the door unlocked." Groan. "Of course, I scaled the tree for photos. I took a few long after the body was carted away." Her eyes tightened but she was still smiling as she fished out her next photo and clipped it to the line. "Any other questions for me, officer?"

Smartypants. "Fine, then tell me who you like for the murder."

Fleur seemed surprised by my question. "Why, Philip, of course," she said. "It has to be him." She leaned one hip against the table, arms crossing like Pamela's, bookending me with journalistic women bent on the truth. "I just got solid confirmation from my FBI contact that Lewis was being paid out of a private fund owned by Blackstone. Made to look like it was a shell owned by protestors." So, Crew's information was out of date? Crap, that wouldn't go over well. "From what I was told, thanks to the federal investigation into his involvement, Lewis lost his usefulness. And someone like him? I wouldn't trust him not to turn on me if you know what I mean."

"You think Lewis was going to talk to the Feds about the deal he made with Blackstone." Pamela didn't sound surprised by Fleur's train of thought.

So, Blackstone had Philip kill him? Then who was Philip talking to on the phone? I wasn't buying it, even if Fleur thought she had the truth nailed down.

Fleur dropped her arms again, returning to her work. As she leaned forward, she exposed a photo that had been hiding behind her, the image making me freeze in place, hitting me almost like a blow.

Pamela noticed my sudden reaction, touched my hand, but I pulled away, backing toward the door. Fleur hissed at me, spinning, then waved for me to just go already. I did, ignoring the tightness of Pamela's expression.

Didn't matter. I had something to check into before I went to Crew and Pamela wasn't invited.

I pulled into the parking lot at *Zip It!*, noting the deputy's cruiser already tucked against the entrance. I knew it was Robert by the terrible parking job, his laziness ensuring he didn't have to walk far to get where he was going. The rest of the lot was empty, the park shut down and I wondered as I slammed my door and headed at a huff for the interior if this place would recover or not.

If Blackstone had anything to say about it? Not likely.

I spotted Robert near the entrance building and headed for him despite having something to look into. I just couldn't pass up the chance to tell him where he could take his sniping childishness. He spotted my approach, mustache quivering, a sneer on his face, gut jutting outward as he rested his hands on his gun belt. I think he realized at the last minute I wasn't slowing down and lost a fraction of his arrogance, a flare of anxiety appearing just before I jabbed him firmly in the chest with one hand, staggering him backward.

Violence was so unbecoming. But I'd had it.

"Listen up, deputy," I snarled. "Your attitude is wearing thin and I'm just about over the harassment you seem to think is appropriate. You cross me one more time and I'll make sure that badge gets shoved down your throat about two seconds after your ass is fired."

He tried to recover, spluttering while the hideous rat on his upper lip quivered but I wasn't done. Not by a long shot.

"You come near me again, you disgusting cretin, and I'll have your ass handed to you before you can blink. You think your mommy can protect you, Robert? Do you?" I pushed him again, knowing I'd gone too far a second after I did it, seeing his rebellion awaken all over again.

"We'll just see who needs protection," he hissed in my face, the stench of his breath making me gag. "When all is said and done, Fiona Fleming, you and that father of yours will regret crossing me."

Whatever that meant. He pushed past me, storming for his car, climbing into the cruiser and driving off in a squeal of tires on the fresh blacktop. Never mind he just abandoned his post, the idiot. Still, as I stood there in the May afternoon, I shivered despite the warmth of the sun, blaming it on the breeze that rose and not my internal worry I might have stirred a hornet's nest.

Nothing to be done about it. I had something I needed to check into before I went to talk to Crew and handed him what he needed to solve this case.

Yes, yes. I should have blah blah blah. Could have yada yada. Surely you know me better than that by now?

I called up the internet on my phone as I hurried into the woods, heading for the tree where the last zip-line began. And squeaked to a halt at the sight of the creeping form of the young man I'd assumed left town already up ahead. He spotted me when I spotted him, his face twisting into a mask of anger. I saw Philip consider running, watching it cross his face, but I was still moving, catching up to him before he could make the choice, tearing the plastic bag from his hand.

Stopping him from dumping the contents onto the ground at the base of the tree he'd chosen for his dirty work.

"Blackstone finally decided to up the ante, I see?" I didn't need to examine the poor little body of the woodpecker in the bag to know what he'd been about to do. Was Robert complicit or was my stupid cousin really as useless as I thought? There was zero doubt in my mind, regardless, that the tiny bird in the bag Philip was about to plant was a red cockaded.

Philip didn't try to take the bag back from me, shrugging, looking away, face pinched with fury. "Things got screwed up," he said. "Left me no choice."

Confirmation of the dead activist's dealings with Blackstone? "Lewis wouldn't plant evidence for you, is that it?" I shook the bag at him. The bastards actually killed an endangered woodpecker to make their plan look legit? That was a new low, though hardly shocking.

His eyes met mine, flicker of irritation there. "I had no contact with that idiot," he said. "Aside from the expected. As far as he knew, I was an activist like him."

Right. Because I knew better now, didn't I? "You had another contact." One I'd seen clearly for the first time in a photo hanging behind Fleur in the *Gazette* dark room.

He didn't respond. "You can't prove anything." He gestured at the bag in my hands. "Your fingerprints are all over that now."

"And your part in Lewis's murder?" I prodded him to see what he'd give me, but Philip instead flashed a horrible, cruel smile.

"I had nothing to do with that," he said. "Good luck trying to prove it. Now, get out of my way before I decide maybe you know too much, and I need to do something about it."

He did not just threaten me. "The sheriff will be in touch," I said, holding up the woodpecker.

"Let him try," Philip said, pushing past me. "Blackstone's lawyers will have something to say about that."

I let him go, heart pounding, staring down at the plastic bag and the little bird, so still and quiet. I could have gone after Philip, but he wasn't my target. And he'd only confirmed what I already suspected, what I'd seen in that photo.

I continued on, the little creature tucked into the pocket of my hoody, renewing my internet search as I moved on. A quick scan of my prompt while I stumbled in the dimness under the foliage, blinking into occasional sunbeams, gave me the information I was looking for, though I stared at it a long moment in shock when it appeared. I clicked through, the image on my screen unexpected but telling as I came to a halt at the base of the tree I'd climbed only a few days ago. I read through the history of the subject in question, surprised to find exactly what I needed to point the finger. Now I just needed one last thing to prove it.

I shivered as I contemplated what I was about to do and tucked my phone into my pocket before starting to climb.

I took my time, scanning the tree's bark, searching for the evidence I wasn't even sure I'd find. It wasn't until I was about halfway to the top, I realized I'd come up here without a helmet or harness. Oh well, I just needed a quick peek, and I was alone, after all. I'd be up and down in a flash and then back on the road to the sheriff's office, hopefully with a scrap of evidence pointing to the murderer. The fact I needed to call Crew crossed my mind, but I was so intent on saving the day—and making him look like a hero—I shrugged off the call until I finished the job I'd started.

Stubborn? Who, me?

The platform awaited, the zip line down on the ground on the far side. I suffered a faint feeling of vertigo, clinging to the side of the tree, grasping the safety cable that held the platform in place with one hand while I searched the bark and branches of the surrounding area, not sure I was going to find what I was looking for but needing to look just in case. Not spotting anything near the platform, I leaned out and peered down, wobbling a bit as the ground seemed to rush toward me while my heart raced.

And my eyes spotted what I'd been seeking. Not believing my luck, I grinned to myself and bent to retrieve it.

At the exact moment someone pushed me from behind.

CHAPTER THIRTY-FOUR

I screamed, clutching reflexively for the safety cable, swinging out over the platform by one hand. I grasped for anything to hold onto with the other, finding and catching a narrow branch while the air left my lungs in a long shriek of terror, the toes of my sneakers scrabbling against the bark and barely catching a hold.

I looked up, doing my best not to swing, fingers already on fire from the pressure of holding most of my body weight, to find Grace standing on the platform, a knife in her hand.

"Please," I whispered, barely able to get that out, the sound soft and pathetic compared to my previous protest. "Please, don't do this." Thirty feet below, the ground waited, beckoned and I had no idea if I could survive such a fall. Really didn't want to find out.

Grace inched forward, face grim, the knife descending toward the safety cable. I couldn't help but whimper as she came closer, her bulky shoes sliding across the wooden surface, the ridged edges familiar. So familiar.

How did I miss that she had such big feet?

"You killed Lewis," I gasped as she reached out to cut the line. My accusation startled her, stopped the descent of her blade. "Why?"

"I saw it in you, the last time we spoke," Grace said. "How close you were to the truth. And that chat you had with Philip." She exhaled abruptly. "If you didn't already know, you were close to the truth. I just needed enough time to think things through." She was sweating, moisture beading on her face. "To turn his death to my advantage. But you're far too smart for your own good, clever girl. That's why I have to kill you." She laughed, though there was no humor in it. "I know your type, Fiona Fleming. Do-gooder who wants the glory for herself. I used to be you." She stopped laughing, gestured at me with the knife. "Lewis wasn't working for Blackstone."

"No," I whispered. "You were."

"I didn't lie to you," Grace said. "You asked about him. Not me."

True enough. I was an idiot. "You sold out. When did he discover you betrayed him?"

Grace's face tightened. "You have no idea." She shifted from one foot to the other. "What it's like. Facing off with corporations like Blackstone and losing over and over again."

"So, you joined them." I couldn't last much longer. If Grace didn't back off, I'd fall even without her threatening knife to finish the job. Why, why didn't I call Crew?

Grace shrugged like it didn't matter. "I need to know what you put together," she said. "What I need to cover up." She jabbed the knife at the line. "Since we're being so open with each other, dear. I've planted more than enough information to mislead that silly journalist." Fleur King. "And even your handsome sheriff." She'd used her Blackstone connection to seed false trails? That was why the confusion between stories. "Not all agents are loyal to that Bureau of his." How deep did the corporation's corruption run?

I didn't want to tell her what I knew, but I had to keep her talking. My life depended on it. I looked down at her shoes and her eyes followed mine, giving me the time to adjust my grip as my fingers slid, sweat making them slick. I sucked in air when my right hand slid over the branch but caught at the end of it, lunging to take a new grip and pulling myself closer to the tree. My toes stayed hooked, my new position making it easier to hang on, to give more pressure over to my feet. Just enough to hold firm another few seconds while Grace looked up and met my gaze again.

"You left a footprint behind," I said. "Along with your protest sign. And the corner of your pocket." The tiny piece of fabric dangled just below me, still hanging from the bark. Close enough in color to the tree itself Jill missed it. But I knew what to look for, didn't I? Especially after seeing that photo of Grace from the gathered crowd, that specific sign in her hands, her intact apparel undamaged. "It wasn't torn before Lewis died." But it certainly was after. She'd worried at the hole in that same pocket while I'd served her tea at the annex, a fresh tear, a bit of dirt circling the hole. Finding the remains of that tear up here meant proof she'd climbed after all. The rest she seemed willing to tell me before she killed me.

She shifted positions again, fingering the hole with her free hand. "Good eyes," she said. "He fought me, and I almost fell. Imagine, he saved me." She laughed again, a barking sound. "Pulled me up after accusing me, after informing me that we were done. That he was leaving me. Told me he forgave me, that he loved me. He *loved* me." She flinched. "I didn't mean to kill him. It was never my intent."

"Not even when he was under investigation by the FBI?" I had to get to the platform somehow. And soon. But Grace wasn't about to move out of the way. "They would have tracked the money back to you, wouldn't they, Grace?" Didn't take a big leap—or much research—to find out she was the treasurer of their little endeavor together.

"He already had." She seemed to collapse a bit in on herself, real sorrow appearing on her face. "That's how he knew it was me. I thought I covered my tracks, but I didn't expect him to go looking. Or for him to put things together, not after all our years as partners." She faltered, hand holding the knife shaking. "I tried to explain." Her face lit with the kind of fervent zeal I'd seen on the first day, her commitment to the cause running deep even now. "That we had to work from inside the system, to save the ones we could and let the others go. But he didn't believe me. He said he loved me. But that he couldn't be with a traitor." She choked on a single sob. "He turned his back on me, was going to tell everyone. I couldn't let him do that."

Never mind she'd set him up to take the fall and left him exposed to the FBI investigation. "You didn't seem to mind putting his reputation at risk." Not to mention his life, in the end. She didn't answer, guilt and what had to be rage flaring in her face. "So, you used the rope you stole from the entry and strangled him with it." She flinched at that mention. Was she reliving what I relived? The bulging eyes, his dying stare? "Why take it in the first place if you didn't intend to kill him, Grace?"

She shrugged. "Always good to have a bit of rope when you climb." That came out absently like she wasn't with me anymore. I hopped my hand up the safety line further, knowing I was on borrowed time.

"You'd know about that," I said. "You used to be a champion climber, once upon a time." The last search of her name turned up her past, with a different surname but the same face, much younger and full of smiles where she hung from the side of a mountain.

Her gaze snapped into focus. "You know about that?"

I nodded. "The internet is deep and holds a lot of secrets." Not sure how I managed to sound so calm while my own life dangled over the edge of a very long drop, fingers and toes going numb. Even if she did back off now, I was pretty sure I couldn't make it to the platform. Funny how the inevitable could wash fear away like nothing else. "I found the records of your awards. Impressive." My fingers trembled, left hand slipping over the thin line. I pulled deep on my reserves and hung on. "You being up here with me now is more than enough proof you had it in you."

She grunted. "No one will believe it," she said. "With you dead?" Whether the fall killed me or not apparently, she planned to finish the job. "I was careful to funnel the money through a fake charity shell company right to Lewis's private account. With the FBI distracted by conflicting stories they can't prove, our activist community will all believe it was Lewis after all, who betrayed them, and I'll carry on as before. The poor dear, poor Grace. They'll follow me with more enthusiasm than they ever did him."

There wasn't much I could say to that. "The corporation wins, then." I swallowed hard as one of my toes slipped, caught. "Blackstone gets this land, and the takeover of Reading begins."

Grace looked startled a moment. "I don't think you get it yet," she said. "Not quite yet. Too bad you won't live to know the full story. But it's not mine to tell and for now, Fiona Fleming, you're out of time."

And then, like it had in the past when my life's

end loomed, the world slowed down to an agonizing pace as Grace leaned forward, knife extended, and cut the safety line to the platform.

One shot, one instant, a single attempt to save my own life. That was all I had in that time between inhale and exhale. I watched her slice, gathered every ounce of strength I had left. And the moment the line parted, I threw myself forward, toes cramping, fingers clutching the branch twisting, my upper body arching as I heaved myself up and over the edge of the platform and caught the lip with my numb fingertips.

My feet couldn't find purchase on the tree, the branch twisting free from my other hand and for a long moment I swung on the tips of my clutching fingers, the sky and the leaves and the open air engulfing me as my pounding heart raged in my head, filling my senses with the thudding beat that was the final sound I would ever hear.

Grace fell to her knees, lunging toward me with her knife outstretched while I swung back, free hand catching at the laces of her ugly man shoes. She cursed as I tugged, jerking her foot out from under her, forcing her to brace herself on the platform, holding up not only her own weight but part of mine as I clung to her foot for dear life.

I was sure his voice calling my name was my mind playing tricks, my need for rescue so deep and terrible I imagined Crew telling me to hold on. Except a moment later he was on the platform, his hands grasping at Grace, Jill right behind him, pinning the woman to the wooden deck while Crew landed on the surface on his stomach, both big hands reaching down to lock around my forearms and jerk me upward in a single, mighty heave. I collapsed beside him, knowing I was sobbing as he rolled over and sat up, pulling me into his lap to cuddle me against his chest and breathe my name into my hair while Jill covered Grace with a scowl and her gun.

"How?" I whispered that question into his ear.

"You can thank Robert," he choked. Never. "For abandoning his post." Aw, hell. "I saw your car, came looking for you."

Damn it. Fine. My jerk of a cousin could have this one.

Meanwhile, as I gathered myself and tried to stop hyperventilating, Crew looked up long enough to glare at the old woman who panted her frustration at the both of us.

"Grace Perkins," he growled, "you're under arrest for the murder of Lewis Brown and the attempted murder of Fiona Fleming."

My hero. Mine. All mine.

CHAPTER THIRTY-FIVE

I stood at the back of the dining room, cheeks aching from the beaming smile I'd worn since the guests started arriving at the annex just this morning, now all seated and watching as one of the stunning brides swept her way to the front of the room, trailing her giant train behind her. Aundrea looked a vision in ivory satin, the ruffled hem of her gown embroidered with colorful flowers that climbed through the overlay of lace weighing down the full skirt. Pamela waited at the top of the makeshift aisle, her simple white suit glowing against her silky blonde bob, matching the sparkle in her eyes as she and her true love finally got their happily ever after.

I dabbed at the tears in the corners of my eyes, sniffling softly to myself, doing my best to stay alert just in case something needed attention without getting totally swept up in the moment. I should have been in the kitchen helping Mom, but even she sat in the front row on the far side with Dad holding her hand, taking a few minutes break from work to watch Pamela Shard marry Aundrea (Patterson) Wilkens at long last.

The discussion about the procession ended abruptly the night before with Pamela putting her foot down and kissing her soon-to-be wife firmly.

"I'm waiting for you," she said. "I've been waiting a long time. I'm done messing around with who's standing where and what we're doing. Just come find me."

Aundrea had laughed, we'd all laughed, and, true to her word, Pamela was there to take her lover's hands in hers while the wedding music swelled and finally came to a halt as the minister began the ceremony.

I had to admit as I looked around the annex dining room looked stunning. The decorators Vivian had recommended did an incredible job, perfection in the guise of Aundrea's favorite flowers, all spring mixes in dazzling hues, adorned the artfully placed giant vases perched almost casually around, piles of more blooms cascading over tables and onto the floor wound through mesh backings that made the room look as if a garden sprung up inside it overnight. The resulting waterfall of blooms filled the space with the heady scent of spring, the breeze washing in through the open doors to the backyard adding that extra, tantalizing promise of summer coming around the corner.

Sunlight poured over the happy couple, cutting past the thin gauze of the curtains over the windows where they'd chosen to say their vows, the stained glass above the tall frames, washing them in as much color as the stunning flowers they'd chosen. Everyone's phones and cameras were out, snapping endless photos, while the tiny, fast figure of the photographer Aundrea hired nipped in and around the gathering to catch the best images. I hadn't been all that surprised to find Fleur departed Reading without saying goodbye, nor that she hadn't stayed for the wedding. I still wondered about her past with Pamela, but it wasn't any of my business. And it was clear from the warm and delighted smile on her face, the journalist had made her heart's choice.

Someone's arms slipped around me, and I hugged Daisy before I knew it was her, the two of us squeezing each other while we sighed in unison over the gorgeous scene.

"Well done, Fee," she whispered in my ear as Pamela said her vows in a clear, strong voice.

"You too, Day," I whispered back. "Partners?"

She giggled in my ear. "You're sure?"

I squeezed harder. "Please, save me from myself."

She hesitated one last second. "Partners," she said with pure delight.

Considering Mom had agreed to the same just yesterday after a long look at my harried and overworked expression, I now had exactly what I was looking for.

Well, not quite. There was one last person I needed a straight answer from. But Crew Turner could wait until after the wedding.

Alicia handed Pamela a ring which she placed on Aundrea's finger. Then it was Jared's mother's turn, her own vows more shakily spoken, enough the gathering in the front tittered their amusement at something I missed. Didn't matter. I'd get the play-by-play from Mom later. Jared, standing with Aundrea, handed off his own ring into his mother's trembling hands and the ceremony came to a quick end with an enthusiastic and heartfelt kiss.

I caught my breath at the sight of Crew as he stood from his seat near the front, following the laughing brides as they came down the aisle toward me. The staff hovered, Daisy ready and waiting, while Mom disappeared back into the kitchen to finish her own preparations. We had exactly one hour to convert the dining room back from wedding hall to somewhere the brides could host their dinner and I wasn't wasting a moment. But I did take that long, happy look at the sheriff—a fresh, crisp haircut adding to his deliciousness—in his dark suit and tie. In that moment I could picture him as the FBI agent he used to be and wondered.

He met my eyes, waited for the bulk of the guests to join the now-married couple in the foyer, then joined me and Daisy while my new partner snapped to work, pulling the doors of the dining room shut, the barrier not quite cutting off her brusque commands. She could be a real general when she needed to be, and I snorted over the sound of her cracking her audible whip.

Crew grinned, towering over me in all his broad-shouldered handsomeness. I'd worn flats instead of heels, knowing how much running I'd be forced to do would make any kind of attempt to augment my height a disaster waiting for my feet to hate me. But that meant he had a serious height advantage, though I wasn't exactly complaining.

Yum.

"Nice wedding," he said. "If you like weddings." What was that sparkle in his blue eyes?

"So far, so good," I said, glancing at the guests mingling and sipping drinks being handed out by a pair of baristas Daisy borrowed from Sammy's Coffee. Olivia's strained smile made me wince as the mayor paused to talk to my dad. He looked uncomfortable in his own suit as if Mom stuffed him into it against his will. The two of them—former sheriff and mayor on the outs—looked far too serious after a moment and parted, frowning.

All I needed was for them to ruin the mood.

"Have to run," I said. "Don't arrest anyone, okay?"

Crew winked, sipping the glass of wine he nabbed from the tray passing by. "No promises."

I wished I could linger and admire him in his suit a little longer, missing for a moment the waves that used to curl over his collar, wondering at the professional cut he'd opted for, thinking about the FBI again. Hopefully, he wouldn't dine and dash and

I'd get the chance to not only feast on the eye candy that was Crew but ask him a few pointed questions about the future. For now, I had the remains of this wedding to survive.

Mom was just as bossy in the kitchen as Daisy was in the dining room, the towering confection of lacy sugar and edible flowers matching the décor perched carefully in one corner, a fence of chairs set around the rolling table Mom built the cake on shielding it from accidental bumps and nudges. I had to admit, it was stunning, six tiers, each one smaller than the last, perched on delicate platforms of glass. I knew from Mom's construction that all six levels held different flavors and that the top tier, simple vanilla cake with cream cheese icing, was Pamela's choice and favorite and would be going home with the couple when the wedding was over.

Dinner went off about as cleanly and hitch-free as I could have hoped for, though when the bread ran out I almost panicked. To my shock, Mom made a rapid call without thinking twice and in twenty minutes a batch of freshly baked rolls and loaves landed in the annex kitchen, the French's Handmade Bakery logo making me itch between my shoulder blades. Not because I begrudged Vivian the business, not in the least. It was more the casual way Mom called on her for help that gave me the heebies.

My suspicions seemed to be coming home to roost and I wasn't all that eager to accept maybe Vivian and I were birds of a feather when it came to my mother.

The guests were happy, that was all I cared about, really. And when Daisy and the staff cleared the last of the food away and Mom wheeled out the cake, the oohs and ahhs of appreciation were totally worth every single moment of angst and struggle it took to get here.

Not just to the wedding day. But the annex, Petunia's, my life. All of it. I inhaled the joy of success, of happiness and my own satisfaction as the couple cut the gorgeous cake.

No one made any jokes about the taste, thank goodness, though I knew from the faint edge to Mom's laughter she had to be thinking about the baking show debacle that almost derailed her. I glanced up as Vivian, an unexpected guest I'd avoided until now, rose from her seat and headed for the foyer, likely looking for the ladies' room, and went after her on impulse.

I caught her almost to the door with the pretty painted woman in the middle, drawing a breath before speaking in the quiet of the hall, the two of us alone for the moment while laughter and the commencement of speeches echoed from the dining room.

"I know what you did." That sounded like an accusation. I cleared my throat to try again while Vivian arched one of her utterly perfect eyebrows at me, her pale ivory dress the exact shade of her blonde hair. Kind of classless in my opinion to wear that color to a wedding, but who was judging?

Me. I was judging. Deep breath, Fee.

"For Mom." That was better. Vivian didn't say anything, just stood there, icy and silent. Waiting. "You canceled the cake order on purpose," I blurted. Look at me, all awkward, just like old times. "You convinced Mom to start baking again." How I had no idea. "You gave my mother her confidence back." That stuck in my throat because Vivian gave Mom what I couldn't. But I wasn't too proud to admit it. "Thank you." There, my voice broke. I hoped she was happy.

Instead of reacting negatively to my weakness, Vivian seemed to soften, just a tiny bit. "Congratulations on the opening of the annex," she said. "And this successful event. I wish you all the best."

I have no idea what moved me, or how I came to be doing it, but an instant after she stopped speaking, I was hugging Vivian, and, shockingly, her arms rose, and she delicately hugged me back.

When I let her go, she met my eyes, hers startled. As she turned and disappeared into the bathroom I didn't follow, turning instead and heading for the kitchen. No way I'd let her see me cry. Or find out I was actually, maybe, starting to respect her.

Nope, not happening.

Sure, Fee. Not at all.

CHAPTER THIRTY-SIX

I hugged Pamela and Aundrea in turn, the pair giggling like little girls as they sank to the surface of the king-sized bed in the honeymoon suite.

"Thank you, Fee," Aundrea said, teary but smiling. "You've made our wedding perfect." She exchanged a loving look with her wife who smiled back.

"Fun times, good food, great friends," Pamela said before winking at me. "Now, get out before you witness something embarrassing."

I grinned as I closed the door behind me, hugging myself in delight as I left the annex to the night staff—I had night staff, imagine—and crossed the yard to Petunia's.

It seemed so quiet in the main house now, though it was as full as ever, spillover guests and my typical business stocking the rooms both upstairs and in the Carriage House. Still, Petunia's had a particularly sleepy feel to it, always had, while I found the energy of the annex much more exciting. Maybe it was the wedding guests? Whatever the reason, I wasn't going to complain or question tonight.

I passed through the kitchen and into the foyer, finding it full of people, faces I knew and adored, for the most part. Crew stood off to one side, leaning against the entry to the sitting room, chatting with Jill. She was out of uniform, dressed in jeans and a tight t-shirt, with Matt standing close enough to her I smirked at myself. Jill waved but didn't stop to talk, leaving a moment later with the ranger holding her hand. Whatever she'd come to tell Crew she'd done her duty and was off to the plans she had for Matt and herself.

No grinning, Fee. Mind your own business.

I watched Olivia shoulder past Geoffrey to hug Mom. "Beautiful cake, Lucy," she gushed. "And the food was extraordinary." Her eyes met mine, but the mayor made no move to come to offer me congratulations. Instead, with a gracious nod to Dad, she turned and left, leaving Geoffrey to watch her go with a barely concealed smirk. He then turned and addressed all of us remaining, as if running for office.

Which he was, clearly.

"Well done and congratulations to Fiona, Daisy and Lucy for such an idyllic wedding." Considering he was married to a Patterson who tried to derail Aundrea's love life in the first place? He could suck it. "I do hope this bodes well for the future of your venture." Wait, how did he know I'd asked Mom and Daisy to partner with me? Grrr. He shook Dad's hand, grinning. "Happy to see you're still ready and able to defend our town, John." Whatever that meant. Dad and I still had a conversation ahead about Blackstone, so defending our town? We'd see about that. "And Sheriff Turner." Geoffrey turned on Crew who straightened slowly from his casual lean, grim expression even more federal agent than previously. "Well done solving yet another horrible crime. Our town owes you a debt."

"Thank Fiona," Crew said without a trace of ego. "She has this knack for murder, it seems."

Thanks a lot.

Geoffrey met my eyes, his cold as a shark, though he continued to smile. "I do hope I can rely on all of you for your support moving ahead." Wow, dude, way to be blatant about wanting Olivia's job. "I'm positive each of you has, as I do, only the best of intentions for Reading at heart."

No one said a word, though Mom huffed softly like she wanted to. Oddly, it was Petunia who got the last word, grumble mumbling at him for standing there like an ass and not paying any attention to her.

Geoffrey glanced down at her, frown taking over his smile before he spun and swept his way out of my B&B while I scowled after him.

I hugged Mom and Dad, happy to see they were smiling, holding hands. They'd mended their fences, apparently, though I'd not been privy to that conversation. Another thing that I needed to keep my nose out of, though they'd forgive me if I held onto a bit of nervous worry they might start fighting again.

They were my parents and I loved them. They weren't allowed to get mad at each other ever again.

Dad kissed my cheek as he and Mom took their leave, though what he whispered left me chilled rather than happy. "Please," he said. "Leave it be." I let him go, knew he referred to Siobhan Doyle and the question I'd asked, not the questions I had about Blackstone. There was too much pain in his voice for the latter.

Surely, he had to know I couldn't do that? I was his daughter, too much a Fleming.

Whoever she was to him? It was time to find out.

Jared poked his nose in from the kitchen, grinning at me, coming to hug me as Daisy said goodbye to Mom and Dad. I embraced him back, feeling bad still for him, but seeing the relaxed look on his face, his real joy for his mother, made me unwind just a bit.

"Carmen and Aiden?" I hated to ask but I needed to know.

He shrugged like he was over it. "She's going to try to make a go of it, I guess," he said. "I told her I'd help after all. Aiden's gone, but he sold his shares to me instead of the Blackstone Corporation, so she's good to go if she wants to."

I shivered a little. "Who are they?" Everything about Blackstone gave me the creeps.

Jared shook his head, frowning a little. "I don't know, Fee. But I'll do everything I can to keep them from buying our town. I promise."

I squeezed his hand. "Grace knew more than she was saying." And she wasn't talking. When Crew brought her in to the station for questioning, me trailing after him still in shock but refusing to go to the hospital until I asked her more about what she knew about Blackstone, the FBI agents waiting there cut off any attempt I could have made to get my answers.

Crew had known them, that much was obvious, and his frustration at their silence told me volumes. The dark-haired woman who paused at the door like she wanted to talk to him decided against it when her gaze met mine and he didn't argue when she left. More history, more secrets to uncover.

As for Philip, he'd been right about the lawyer thing. Crew's attempts to track and interrogate the liaison were hit hard with so many layers of men in dark suits from Blackstone's letterhead he backed off, though I could tell it frustrated him to no end.

Jared hugged me again. "I just wanted to thank you for giving Mom and Pamela their perfect day." He winked down at me. "There might be another wedding coming up in the near future, so promise me you'll give us the same treatment when I figure out if Alicia will say yes before I ask her."

I laughed in pure delight, kissed his cheek. "Idiot," I whispered. "She'd marry you right now if you wanted. Don't let her go."

He met my eyes, his damp and cleared his throat, voice thick when he spoke. "Great idea," he said, and exited back into the kitchen. I just hoped he had a ring in one of his pockets or she'd kick his butt.

When I turned back around to say goodbye, Daisy squeezed me out of the blue.

"Love you," she whispered before arching an eyebrow. Then, with a breezy wave for Crew, she vanished out the front door and closed it softly behind her.

Leaving us alone together, aside from the quietly humming pug who looked back and forth between me and the sheriff as if anticipating something even I wasn't sure about.

I met his blue eyes, held my breath. "Do you miss it?" Um, why was I asking him this now? And could I be a bit vaguer? But he seemed to understand what I meant because Crew shrugged.

"I chose a different road when I left the Bureau and California," he said, closing the distance between us, smiling, waiting. "One that led me to you."

Long exhale. "Would you like to come downstairs?" Fiona Fleming. Giggle.

His smile was the correct response, though when he took my hand and led me to the door to my apartment, that was kind of perfect, too.

CHAPTER THIRTY-SEVEN

I passed him a beer, Petunia whining for a treat beside the open fridge door. I sighed and handed her a fist full of blueberries while Crew cracked his drink. I turned back to find him shedding his jacket, tossing it on the sofa, rolling up his sleeves and discarding his tie, the top two buttons on his white dress shirt undone before he took a long drink of his beer.

His eyes never left mine.

Oh, my goodness.

I fought for a breath as I sipped from my own bottle, suddenly nervous and so close to giggles I really needed to get a grip already. But it had been a long, long time and the last man I trusted betrayed me to the core of my heart. And yet, despite it all, here I was, willing to trust again. Mind you, Ryan Richards had nothing on Crew Turner.

Just saying.

Crew closed the distance between us, setting down his beer bottle, blue eyes distracted by something on the counter next to me. He came to an abrupt halt while my poor heart went pitter-pat and tried to exit out my feet at the sharp look of shock on his face. When I glanced toward the object of his newfound attention, I realized he was staring at the cover of *The Reading Hoard: Fact or Fiction.*

Huh. What was that all about?

I laughed a little to lighten the mood. "Daisy and I stole it from the library. Just a little pet project we're working on."

My words seemed to break him out of his surprise, though when he started moving again, he didn't hug me or kiss me or even look at me. Instead, to my (irritation) surprise he instead retrieved the book, holding it carefully and almost reverently in his hands. My eyes drifted from the crinkled plastic protecting the cover to the tattoo on his wrist and, on impulse, I reached out and traced it with my fingertips.

Crew looked up, blue eyes full of something I couldn't read. "My grandfather had the same tattoo," he said, voice husky with emotion. Sorrow? "And my dad." Definitely loss. I didn't need to ask for more information. He started talking and kept going, almost too fast for me to keep up. "I got mine when Dad was diagnosed with Alzheimer's." His fingers clenched around the book. "To feel closer to him, to my past." He laughed then, still sad but full of a kind of wonder that made him look younger than Jared. "I've been in Reading before, Fee, did you know that?" He didn't stop staring at the book. "I even stayed at Petunia's, with my father. I met you, once. I remember you." He finally met my eyes. "As a little girl. All that red hair and your temper. You told me off for picking a flower from your grandmother's garden. I think I was ten?"

Holy, what did he just say? I wished I recalled, could remember him, too, the instant of our first meeting, but I couldn't despite myself.

Crew didn't seem to care, gaze locking on the cover once more. "Granddad said we were descended from Captain Reading." Another laugh, bright but brittle this time. "After Mom died, Dad brought me here that summer. To look for the treasure, he said. But more to spend time with me, maybe. We both missed her so much. This was just a family joke." He held up the book, turned it to face me, tears in his blue eyes. "Alistair Markham was my grandfather. I moved here, took this job after Michelle died, because I wanted to be close to my family, if only their memory. That's how I ended up in Reading." He set the book aside, retrieved his beer, but didn't move while my entire body shivered.

Choke. Splutter. No way.

I couldn't breathe, couldn't think. And then I was moving, faster than I should have been under the circumstances considering my lack of ability to focus on actually making forward progress without hurting myself, tripping over Petunia and hissing an apology to her when she yipped in protest but unable to slow down. I didn't stop until I skidded to a halt at my bedside, lifting the music box in my hands which I carried at a near run to the kitchen counter, met with Crew's renewed surprise.

My fingers trembled when I fumbled the lid open, let the song play, revealed the secret compartment. Lifted out the scrap of the map my grandmother left me and held it up, the thin parchment shivering in my grasp.

Crew stared a long moment, the beer bottle thudding to the counter, sliding from his loosened touch. An instant later his own hand slid into his back pocket as if of its own volition, retrieving his wallet. And, from the folds of black leather, he pulled out a scrap of his own, pressing the edges of the aged ivory paper into the torn side of mine until the partial compass was complete.

Our eyes met and I giggled, chest tight with the need to collapse in hysterics. "Crew," I whispered, fumbling the doubloon out onto the counter, the gold singing as the coin spun its final way to quiet.

"Fee," he said. "It *can't* be."

"But it has to," I said. "The hoard. Your grandfather, your father, my grandmother. They all had pieces. They all knew the truth."

He hugged me suddenly, kissing me before letting me go, more joy in him than I'd ever seen before.

"It's real," he said. "The Reading hoard is real and it's here." Crew's blue eyes shone as he laughed out loud. "And we're going to find it."

The Reading
Reader Gazette

VOLUME 1   ISSUE 1   MAY 14TH, 2019   WWW.RRGAZETTE.COM

News Briefs

1. **Yacht Club Mixer:** The Reading Yacht Club Mixer will be held at the Yacht Club on Saturday, August 17th from 7-10PM with dance to follow. VIP tickets available at town hall or through Isaac at the club office. Support your local club, get your tickets now!

2. **Parking Violations:** Your town council would like to remind you that parking restrictions are ongoing this summer. Due to increased tourist activity, a year-round ban on street parking will be firmly enforced. Please note, violations have been ticketed and fines will be pursued. Any Reading resident whose vehicle is found parked outside their driveway will be towed at their expense. The sheriff's department asks you to please park responsibly. Let's keep Reading's streets safe!

3. **Cutter Lake Contamination:** It has come to the attention of council that there's been an increase in bacterial culture in our very own Cutter Lake. While measures are being taken to ensure the safety of swimmers in our beautiful natural resource, all residents are asked to please obey signage and remain out of the water for the duration of testing. Boats are, of course, exempt from this rule. Thank you!

4. **Vandalism Courtesies:** While likely pointing to whoever insists on defacing the statue of our town founder, would whoever or the budding artist is please just stop. We're tired of the mess. Measures are being taken to film the area, so if you think you're safe from prosecution, we know who you are.

Winner of this week's Fire Hall 50-50 draw: Alice Moore. Congratulations, Alice!

Please send any pending community notices to: pamela@rrgazette.com before 4PM

Deadly Protest Ends in Murder

Grace Perkins, 64, of Woods, NC, is in FBI custody for the murder of her partner, renowned activist Lewis Brown.

Activist extinct after stunning act of betrayal

By Pamela Saard

Well-known and respected environmental activist, Lewis Brown, 85, of Devon, WI, was found strangled early this week while leading a protest in the *Zip It!* zip line park. The newly opened facility was the scene of his untimely demise at the hands of his partner and long-time girlfriend, Grace Perkins, 64.

This paper is unable to report on her motives as we have been served with a gag order courtesy of Blackstone Corporation pending her arraignment. Though arrested initially by our very own Sheriff Crew Turner, she was quickly whisked from Reading in the company of several agents of the Federal Bureau of Investigation, none of whom would comment nor supply their names or badge numbers.

The tragic death of Lewis Brown has been buried by government officials and lawyers representing Blackstone Corporation, leaving this journalist with no recourse but to speculate instead of reporting the news.

It should be noted that our own Fiona Fleming was yet again instrumental in not only uncovering the murder victim but in revealing the identity of the perpetrator, putting her very life at risk for our town once again in her pursuit of justice.

Meanwhile, Mayor Olivia Walker refuses to comment on anything to do with this incident, though it's come to the attention of the Gazette that local accountant and Patterson son-in-law, Geoffrey Jenkins, has decided to run against her for mayor in the coming fall election.

With a string of murders behind us and uncertain leadership ahead, this reporter will be looking to the shifting hands of the political scope in Reading while wondering just who might be pulling the strings in our fair town.

For now, *Zip It!* continues operation under the ownership of Carmen Martinez and local construction company CEO Jared Wilkins. The Reading Corporate Retreat Initiative, brainchild of Mayor Walker, remains in full swing, attracting visitors from around the

272

Looking for more Fiona Fleming?
Find book seven, ***Anchors Away and Murder***
available now!

AUTHOR NOTES

MY DARLING READER:
I'm so in love with Fee and Crew, with the story of their connection, and I'm so delighted to finally get to share some of his backstory at last.

The voices I write for, especially the long series characters, tend to love to lead me down these endless and convoluted roads, unwinding treasures of the emotional and mysterious kind, over the course of many books and multiple hints. Crew's past is no exception, nor is his tie to Fee and the treasure they both seek.

For those of you dying to know, who are as deeply invested in the threads of mystery running beneath the town of Reading as much as the individual cases Fee and Crew investigate, I offer you a whisper of giddy excitement. As I finished the writing of this book, Fee finally told me how everything ends. And just how perfectly it links back to the beginning.

I can't wait for you to find out more, because the suspense is killing me.

Best,
Patti

ABOUT THE AUTHOR

EVERYTHING YOU NEED TO know about me is in this one statement: I've wanted to be a writer since I was a little girl, and now I'm doing it. How cool is that, being able to follow your dream and make it reality? I've tried everything from university to college, graduating the second with a journalism diploma (I sucked at telling real stories), am an enthusiastic member of an all-girl improv troupe (if you've never tried it, I highly recommend making things up as you go along as often as possible) and I get to teach and perform with an amazing group of women I adore. I've even been in a Celtic girl band (some of our stuff is on YouTube!) and was an independent film maker (go check out the Lovely Witches Club at www.lovelywitchesclub.com). My life has been one creative thing after another—all leading me here, to writing books for a living.

Now with multiple series in happy publication, I live on beautiful and magical Prince Edward Island (I know you've heard of Anne of Green Gables) with my multitude of pets.

I love-love-love hearing from you! You can reach me (and I promise I'll message back) at patti@pattilarsen.com. And if you're eager for your next dose of Patti Larsen books (usually about one release a month) come join my mailing list! All the best up and coming, giveaways, contests and, of course, my observations on the world (aren't you just dying to know what I think about everything?) all in one place: http://smarturl.it/PattiLarsenEmail.

Last—but not least!—I hope you enjoyed what you read! Your happiness is my happiness. And I'd love to hear just what you thought. A review where you found this book would mean the world to me—reviews feed writers more than you will ever know. So, loved it (or not so much), your honest review would make my day. Thank you!

Made in United States
North Haven, CT
29 August 2024

56676187R00153